The Honey Bee Girl

ISBN: 1-4196-3067-9

To order additional copies, please contact us.
BookSurge, LLC
www.booksurge.com
1-866-308-6235
orders@booksurge.com

DOUG
HISER

THE HONEY BEE GIRL

2006

The Honey Bee Girl

CREDITS

"Snow White" by Anne Sexton
KISS the rock band
The Houston Astros
Tabasco by E.A. McIlhenny
Falstaff Beer
Johnny Cash
Merle Haggard
Tom T. Hall
Loretta Lynn
Dolly Parton
Carlsbad Caverns
"The Tar Baby" by Uncle Remus
"Tarzan" by E.R. Burroughs
Galveston County Fair and Rodeo
Sea Arama Marine Park
"Godzilla" by Tomoyuki Tanaka
Genesis the rock band
Sly and the Family Stone
The "Gor" novels by John Norman
Dairy Queen
"Underdog" by Total Television
Greyhound Dog Track
"The Three Stooges" by C3 Entertainment, Inc.
"Superman" by D.C. Comics
"Spiderman" by Marvel Comics and Stan Lee
"Green Goblin" by Marvel Comics and Stan Lee

"Cinderella" by Charles Perrault
"Annie's Song" by John Denver
Rudyard Kipling
Robert Cochrane
Robert Browning
"The Tiger" by William Blake
"The Fox and the Crow" Aesop's Fables
"The Cloud" by Percy Bysshe Shelley
"The Wizard of Oz" by Frank L. Baum
"Black Dog" by Led Zeppelin
"Love Rollercoaster" by The Ohio Players
The Doobie Brothers
The Moody Blues
The Galveston Daily News
PBS channel 8
National Geographic
Jethro Tull

This book is for Kathy Brotherton and the City of Santa Fe, Texas

"I love the spirit of Santa Fe, southern Texas small towns, fresh hay, tall grasses, tallow trees, crawfish castles, and the way your hair blows in the wind like a horse's mane. And I love holding hands with you in the pastures of my youth." Driving Slow: <u>Lost Oasis</u> by Doug Hiser

"She is a drug, she is a nymph, she is jungle and darkness, she is the first taste of whiskey…And the gut burn." <u>Whisky Moon</u> by Doug Hiser

"Let's go to Oz. A cool place where everyone can wear red shoes."
The Jets Roar:
<u>Shards of Lies</u> by Doug Hiser

"All I wanted was to live forever in her arms. All I wanted was her love. Reality soaks me like gasoline…Please don't drop that match."
<u>Lost Oasis</u> by Doug Hiser

"I learned to walk in cowboy boots...Found it made my legs sturdy."
Lost Oasis by Doug Hiser

BOOKS BY DOUG HISER

Shards of Lies
The Seven Rured Embrace
Whiskey Moon
Bite of the Mailman
Secret Grotto
Lost Oasis
Cavern of the Eggstone
Crow Canyon
Wink-Eye Creek
Cover Art by Doug Hiser

INTRODUCTION

The older you get the smaller the world gets. When you are a kid the cow pastures stretch for hundreds of miles and sometimes you never get to explore their farthest edges. What is not explored is mystery. Without mystery the world would be boring.

This novel takes place in Santa Fe, a real town in Texas, and even though this is a work of fiction it is based on many factual events that took place in my life in 1972 and 1973. Please remember that this is fiction, even if there is much truth between the lines. Growing up in a small town in Texas was hard for someone like me: an artist and a writer, a creative person. I molded my personality to fit in with the athletes and the cowboys. I knew I was always different because of my imagination. I loved the outdoors, exploring the wild land behind our house, catching snakes, turtles, and chasing cottontail rabbits through the tall grass, and building secret forts in the sticker brush. I would rather be wading through a pond, grabbing catfish by the tail than inside watching the television, like so many of our kids today.

I wrote this novel because of a profound effect that a young girl had on me back then. Her name was Kathy Brotherton. She moved to Santa Fe to live with her dad and she was an enigma to me then and now. This book is dedicated to her.

"1972"

When I was fifteen years old I caught a marsh hawk using my bare hands and an empty feed sack. The hawk had a broken wing and had fallen into a ditch near the rice canals. A bullet had shattered the hawk's wing bone. I knew the marsh hawk would never fly over the south Texas rice fields and canals again. I tried to mend the wing with tape and gauze, as best I could figure out from my bird book. Trying to keep the raptor fed with small birds that I shot with my BB rifle was a daily task. Each afternoon I watched the marsh hawk pounce, with one good wing across his chicken coop, on top of a dead sparrow or field lark. The hawk lived in captivity but he never flew again. I cared for that marsh hawk and hoped to see it fly again but there are some things not destined to heal. This lesson would be repeated for me in more serious circumstances, as I grew older.

"I USED TO KNOW A GIRL WITH BLUE-GREEN EYES,"

I used to know a girl with blue-green eyes, the kind of blue-green eyes that are surrounded by a thin black ring. The kind of blue-green eyes that seemed like a far away ocean roared on rocky shores within their depths. I remember how beautiful she looked. She was beautiful the way a morning glory's petals open and attract honeybees like a grand aurora borealis of pollen and color. I can still see her in my mind, golden legs striding through the tall wheat grass as she walked far out in the hay fields. She would sit all alone, picking flowers and seed puffs. I remember the way her dark blonde hair moved in the wind and of how I could never approach her.

The trees and the people in southern Texas are similar. They grow strong and straight and put down deep roots, staying in the same place their entire lives, never wandering far from the area. Rae was different. She was more like a leaf blown by the breeze across the pastures, tumbling and rolling, maybe like a seed puff carried by the wind, never staying long enough anywhere to plant those roots. Rae followed the wind, searched the zephyrs for different answers, and never belonged in the forest.

I was a sophomore in high school and she was a freshman. I was small for my age but athletic and quick. My hair was light brown but sun-bleached blonde on top. My Dad called me cotton-top because my hair reminded him of a cotton-tailed rabbit. Last summer she had moved to our town, Santa Fe, Texas. The town was tiny, only a black dot on a folded out Texas map. She was small and skinny with pink lips that reminded me of a slice of wet watermelon on a hot summer's day. I used to stretch out on the top of our tin barn and just watch her in the fields as she sat there in the tall grass. I often wondered what she thought about, sitting out there by herself for hours, but I was always too shy to even speak to her on an intimate level.

Her name was Rae Kimmings. Her parents, Joshua and Katherine Kimmings, had moved here to Texas from Durango, Colorado. Mr. Kimmings was transferred from his job or something like that. They bought the only other house on my dead end street. Rae never fit in at the Santa Fe High School. She only had a couple of friends and they were the weirdest kids in the school, Jade Morgan and Leslie Gertone. Jade was an overweight girl with flat black hair and she always wore black clothing. Rae's other friend, Leslie, was into every type of drug that existed, which is why her face always had bad acne. She was as thin as a hunger-strike rebel. Jade also did drugs but mostly she was an alcoholic, preferring Jack Daniels whiskey, instead of weed. Both girls slept around with anyone and everyone. Some of my friends had even been with them. I had never seen the attraction but then when people get stupid drunk anything can happen and usually does. I never drank alcohol back then because I was afraid of losing control, even now I rarely drink. I still like to keep that control.

Rae was the most introverted girl I had ever known. I guess she became friendly with those two wild renegades because Rae did like to smoke weed. When I found out that she smoked the stuff I was sort of hurt because it tarnished this beautiful picture that I had conjured up of her inside my mind. I never actually saw her smoke but I knew she did. A lot of guys were interested in Rae when she first came to Santa Fe but she wasn't interested in any of them. Rumors even went around the town that she liked girls, that she was a lesbian. I didn't believe any of those stories. Rory Marks kept telling everyone that he seen her with Sharleen Little, a lesbian woman who was about thirty and lived in the Santa Fe Buzzy Bee Trailer Park. He said he seen them naked through the window of her trailer and they were kissing and touching. Rory Marks was also embarrassed because she had turned down his constant pursuing. Once she told him to leave her alone and that she just wasn't interested in a muscle-head football jerk. She said this right in front of a group of the cheerleaders. I never believed anything about Rae, except the stuff about her smoking weed. She was a mystery and lived in different world than all the people that I knew.

The first time I saw Rae up close I was stunned by her eerie blue-green eyes and those pouty pink lips. I was walking down my gravel road when I noticed Mr. Kimmings dragging something out of the back of his pickup truck. I walked up his driveway to get a better look and asked, "Need any help?"

He was a big broad shouldered guy with a geeky-looking handlebar mustache and he turned and smiled, "Sure buddy, grab a handle and help me get this tub out."

I ran up and grabbed a handle of the big tub and glanced inside as we lowered it to the ground. The tub was full of dead snapping turtles. I had never seen so many snapping turtles all at once. To me those turtles were like rare prehistoric creatures just discovered on odd occasions. I had only caught a few of them and I knew how dangerous they could be. They had long sharp claws and could even climb chicken wire with their sharp beaks and long claws. My Dad told me once that if a snapping turtle bit you that it wouldn't let go until it rained.

The scariest thing about snapping turtles is their long neck. Most turtles that I had caught were not very dangerous and you could just hold them by their shells and then they couldn't bite you but snapping turtles had these very long necks all hidden inside their shells. If you didn't know any better you would just try to grab a snapping turtle by the back of his shell and pick it up. I found out real quick about that big mistake. I almost lost the fingers on my right hand the first time I tried to pick up one like that. The turtle's long neck shot out of the shell and arched backwards over it's back, snapping it's sharp beak, barely missing my fingers. I quickly dropped the scary turtle back into the water. I found out later that the only way to safely handle one of those snapping turtles is to hold it by the end of it's long jagged tail and to keep it held away from your body.

I was curious as to why Mr. Kimmings had a tub full of dead ones and so I asked, "What are you gonna' do with all these dead turtles?"

He smiled and showed his yellow cigar smoke-stained teeth and said, laughing, "We're gonna' eat 'em. My wife is gonna' fix a delicious turtle soup."

I thought that was gross but I didn't say anything. I kept the conversation going and asked, "How did you catch all them turtles?"

"I put out stringer lines last night all down the canal. I caught some catfish too. The fish are over there in the ice chest. One is huge, about fifteen pounds. Channel cat. I think I'm gonna' have a big neighborhood fish fry and invite everybody."

"Mr. Kimmings, next time you go turtle fishing you think that I could go?"

"Sure, as long as your parents don't mind. Hey, you want to help me clean these turtles and catfish?"

I followed him to the backyard as he carried the ice chest. We went back and carried the tub full of dead snapping turtles together. Mr. Kimmings went in the garage and returned with a huge knife. I watched him cut off the turtle's heads and then he peeled back their shells and I could see all their guts and stuff. The smell was almost overpowering, a stink nearly as bad as a dead skunk but more musty. It was fascinating but kind of made me feel sick. I was standing there, the turtle eyes all popping out; watching him cut up the dead turtles when out of the house came Rae. She was wearing very short white shorts and a white halter-top. Her tan legs moved so gracefully and I could even see the tiny blonde hairs on her upper thigh where the razor had stopped. I completely forgot about the dead turtles. I had seen this girl only from a distance before now and being this close to her was overwhelming. She was the prettiest girl I had ever encountered. Her long dark blonde hair was pulled back and held by a plastic flower and I noticed her slender neck and the smooth skin on which her gold chain rested. She stopped abruptly, not expecting to see me in her backyard and then her face resumed its normal mysterious blankness as she said to her father, "Dad, Mom said to tell you that she is going to the store. Do you need anything?"

He just grunted and didn't even look up from his work, "No."

She looked at the chopped-up dead turtles and wrinkled her nose at the gross smell. Rae looked at me and made a weird face and then turned around and ran into the house like an aloof deer, too proud to even get a drink of water, afraid to cause ripples in it's reflection. At least that is what I thought about her personality on that first meeting.

Rae was an obsession for me in a strange way. She wasn't always on my mind but if I saw her everything else stopped.

Nothing mattered but Rae. I rarely even talked to her except for small talk, usually about her parents and stuff about the neighborhood. I never could figure her out. She was such a beautiful girl but she acted like a strange creature that lived in the lost woods without a connection to society.

"...YOU BETTER WATCH OUT FOR THE BEES."

One day I was walking down my road, going past her house and I noticed her sitting in her front yard in a big patch of clover. The little white clover flowers were all around her and I could see many honeybees buzzing and landing on the flowers. She held a small book in her hands. I had never seen anyone sit outside on the ground and read books before. I immediately thought that this was kind of 'cool'. I also thought this would be a good opportunity for me to begin a conversation with her.

I walked through the ditch in her front yard and she looked up to see me approaching. She wrinkled her eyebrows down and I waited for a smile but she just squinted a bit and then returned her gaze to the book. I would have turned around and left but I was already committed so I said, "Hi, Rae. What are you reading?"

She didn't even look up but she said, in almost a whisper, "Poetry."

Rae's voice was very soft and even when she spoke normally it seemed you had to stretch your ears to hear her. I thought it had something to do with her shyness. At the time I had never even read any poetry in my life and was lost on how to continue the conversation. I tried anyway. "Rae, it sure is a nice day. That clover looks really comfortable but you better watch out for the bees."

She looked up from her book and our eyes met. I don't mean staring only just for a second because we held each other's eyes for a long time. That was the first time she had ever really let me see deep into her. Looking into her eyes like that made me want to cry for her. I could sense so much sadness and pain. I didn't understand where it came from or even why it was there but I knew Rae was the saddest person I had ever met just by looking into her eyes that time. She looked away finally, looking directly into the south wind and her hair flew out behind her like peacock's fan. She said, in that soft voice, "The bees are my friends."

I was still standing up and I decided it was okay to sit down in the clover beside her. As I started to sit down she said, "Don't sit on any of the little flowers."

I sat next to her, positioning myself in an area where I didn't mash any of the flowers and my left knee was barely touching her right knee. I was more conscious of that tiny contact with Rae than I would have been if a bee had stung my butt at that moment. She turned her head slightly and began to read, "No matter what life you lead the virgin is a lovely number: cheeks as fragile as cigarette paper..." She continued to read the pages to me in that soft whispery voice and I watched her pink lips as they perfectly pronounced each word, each syllable. She was incredibly intelligent but I knew that she did terrible in school. Rae was ambiguous and perplexing, exciting and odd. I listened and observed her beauty. "Meanwhile Snow White held court, rolling her china-blue doll eyes open and shut and sometimes referring to her mirror as women do." She looked up from the open book and asked, with a tiny smile revealing small dimples in her cheeks and I had never noticed before, "Do you know what that poem was about?"

I really had missed most of it because I had been thinking about her so I said, stupidly, "Yes."

She just stared at me and I continued, "It was about Snow White."

Rae laughed, and flashed those dimples and her eyes glowed. She reached across and grabbed my arm, shaking me playfully, and said, "Snow White? Yeah, you're right." She winked and said, "Do you know who wrote the poem?"

I was on a roll and she was actually holding my arm. Electric shocks were crackling up my arm into my body and I wanted to kiss her and the shocks were like lightning into my heart that kept beating and beating, faster and faster. I looked deep into her eyes and said, "Walt Disney."

The spell was broken. She let go of my arm and stopped laughing. I didn't know how to react. She was quiet and then after an awkward silence she finally said, in a far away voice that seemed to come to me on the wind from a hidden cave under the sea, "Anne Sexton wrote that poem in 1971. She is my favorite poet."

I really didn't know what to say because I was still trying to understand what had happened to her mood when I watched her pick a little clover flower with a honeybee perched on the flower. She lifted the flower to her face, the bee only inches from her nose, and she blew a breath of air on the flower and the bee. The honeybee flew up a few inches and was hovering right in front of her eyes. I was mesmerized. The honeybee hovered there for a few seconds and then flew directly at me. I jumped backwards and thrust my hands at it. I could hear it buzzing about my head and I stumbled to my feet and jumped around in a circle. Finally I stopped jumping and the bee was gone. I looked at Rae but she was reading her poetry book and not watching me. I walked home feeling embarrassed and confused.

"...THE INDIAN RODE A HORSE AROUND THE FOOTBALL FIELD..."

Our little town of Santa Fe is sort of famous or infamous these days, depends on which way you look at the situation. The town called "The City of Santa Fe" had a court case go all the way to the Supreme Court and it made national headlines. The case was about whether the town had a right to say a prayer before high school football games. At first I heard they won the right to pray and then I heard they didn't so as far as I know, people still pray if they want to. Santa Fe was also infamous for burning books and passing out Bibles to children during school. It seems the place has become a war ground for religious beliefs. Another claim Santa Fe has to news is the persistent rumors that the place is an active Ku Klux Klan stronghold. I do recall the Klan holding a large meeting out in someone's cow pasture many years back. I remember people got on the local television news holding rifles and burning crosses. I think the entire episode had something to do with the Asian community shrimping the waters a few miles away in Kemah, Texas. The fishermen who have lived there for generations were upset about the Asians coming in and competing with them for the shrimp. Those are the few things I know of "The City of Santa Fe."

That is the Santa Fe of recent years. The place actually was three small towns all combined into the Santa Fe school district during the time Rae and I were growing up. The school was called Santa Fe because the main highway that connected all three towns, State Highway 6, ran parallel to the Santa Fe Railroad tracks. The school mascot was an Indian. The Santa Fe Indians are what they are still called. There was once a time when the Indian rode a horse around the football field when the football team scored a touchdown. Those days are gone because the high school football powers of the U.I.L. ruled it against their commanding rules. The Indian mascot has an origin also and that brings me to the three small towns along highway 6, between Hitchcock and Alvin.

Alta Loma, Arcadia, and Algoa, three separate but connected towns. Alta Loma is Karankawa Indian for "high ground." The Karankawa Indians lived in these areas and in Galveston before the area of Texas was settled. Alta Loma was the largest and most inhabited town of the three and the center for business, pharmacy, gas stations, the water company, and the feed store. Arcadia and Algoa were less populated. All three towns combined have a large land area because of the many huge cattle ranches. During my teen years; the population was dominated by Italian families; mostly with descendents living on Galveston Island.

The town has always been generally farm and ranch people but during the last ten years people have been moving away from the bigger cities and settling in Santa Fe. Santa Fe is only about a twenty to thirty minute drive from the largest city in Texas, Houston. Many of the people began moving south to avoid the cluster of the big city in preference of small country living. The town life has changed and the religious wars have taken over the populace. Once a heavy catholic influence now the town has almost every religion trying to dominate the people with its own agenda. The church populations of the Baptists and the Pentecostals, the Charismatic and the

Christians, the Holy Rollers and the Lutherans, and on and on, all competed for their small piece of your pocket book and your soul. The little town Rae and I lived in, once upon a time, is gone, and I truly miss it.

There is an unusual ancient looking castle built in the middle of Alta Loma, along Highway 6. I have heard several stories about the castle. I don't know if this is true or not but the most often told story is that the Godfather of the Mafia had built the castle. He built this castle back when Galveston had casino gambling and was known as "Little Las Vegas." During that time Alta Loma didn't exist and he built a dirt road, leading twenty-six miles out of Galveston. Along this dirt road he built the castle for his mistress. He had his own private getaway from the fast times of Galveston, twenty-six miles away in the country, with his mistress.

Different families had owned the castle over the years, and once it was even turned into an apartment complex. I actually went to high school with a girl who lived in one of the apartments. I have also heard at times that it was haunted but I have no proof of any of those stories that were probably made up to scare kids away. The castle looked scary enough without ghost stories.

The castle was surrounded on three sides by thick forest trees and huge honeysuckle plants. One night my brother, Jerry, and my cousin, Kenny, and the guy across the street, Terry, had decided to sneak into the woods behind the castle. We wanted to camp out behind the castle all night. The castle was about five miles from our houses on Bunde Street. We rode our bikes, starting out at dusk loaded down with packs full of Twinkies, chips, and Cokes, to the castle. Hiding the bikes in the deep weeds by the ditch that ran along side of the highway, we crept quietly around the side of the castle. At this time an

Italian family owned the place. I heard the owner was a very nasty man with a big chest and a temper to match. The main reason we wanted to camp near the castle was because of the story I heard told that day.

Richard Chunbartio, a plump freckled kid told me the story of the howling ghost that haunted the castle. I was afraid of ghosts but their existence always intrigued me. It was like a feeling of something hidden inside when the fear creeps throughout your body. The feeling is better explained by an example of an anthill. An anthill is a peaceful mound of dirt in the pasture. The hill is serene and smooth, usually with no sign of any activity on the outside. Inside the anthill we know that there are millions of ants, working, eating, and doing ant duties. Thrust your hand into the anthill and the peaceful serenity is gone. The ants will explode out of the mound and cover your hand in seconds, inflicting stings like burning electric shocks. You will feel intense pain the longer you leave your hand there. The ants are enraged and battle to the death. The ant mound is the example of your calm mind and the explosion of ants is the realization of the sensation of true fear, the numbing, unknown, livid kind of fear.

We had crept through the tall weeds and brush of the surrounding area near the back of the castle. We tried to be as quiet as possible and at one point we just stopped and listened intently. The brush was quiet. We could only hear our own breathing. I was behind Kenny and Terry. I was about to take another step, when I noticed something moving by my shoe. It was dark and I couldn't tell what it was at first, but I knew it was some sort of small animal. I thought it was a cat but then I could see it better and I knew what it was. It wasn't a cat. I had to clench my teeth from hollering and dashing off past Kenny and Terry. It was a skunk. I didn't want to get sprayed by the skunk so I stood perfectly still to avoid any threatening movements towards the animal. Skunk musk is so powerful you have to burn your clothes afterwards. We once had a big bull-mastiff dog that used to run skunks down and kill them. He would bring them home and leave the dead skunks on the front porch like some bizarre trophy. The dog's name was Tiger and I don't know why because he wasn't striped or orange at all. Tiger loved to kill skunks and I guess he was impervious to their deadly odor. We would bathe him and bathe him but the odor lingered for days after a skunk killing. Tiger was a good dog, except for his skunk killing habits, and we kept him for many years until he died one day. I don't know why he died but we never had another dog that killed skunks.

I liked the jeans I had on and I didn't want to bathe in tomato juice a hundred times with my Mom scrubbing my skin off so I wanted to avoid being sprayed by the inquisitive skunk. Kenny and Terry had continued walking and were getting farther away from the skunk and I. Finally I saw that Kenny looked back. He yelled in a whisper, "Why are you stopping?"

I couldn't say anything because the skunk was still sniffing at my shoe. Terry heard Kenny and he stopped too. They both motioned me to come with them but I couldn't move or say anything. They thought that I was scared and made faces at me. The skunk started chewing on my shoe. I thought to myself, maybe I could kick him like a football before he could spray me. I could just imagine the skunk flying through the air past Kenny and Terry, spraying them as he went over their heads. I almost laughed out loud at my thoughts. Kenny loudly whispered back at me, "Hurry up! Get going! It isn't that scary!"

Kenny turned and continued walking away from me. I

felt abandoned but I wasn't afraid of the dark or the weeds and stickers I stood in. I just wanted to be still and not get sprayed by the skunk chewing on my shoe. Terry and Kenny were leaving me behind without looking back and I watched the skunk finally get bored with my shoe and scamper away into the brush. I waited a few seconds and then jumped and half ran, half hopped over sticker bushes trying to catch up with Terry and Kenny. I made a lot of noise catching up with them and they told me to be quiet as I finally trotted up behind them. We were about twenty-five yards behind the castle now. We stopped and stared at the large dark building. It was ominous and surreal. The castle looked so out of place here in this grove of oak trees and flat cow pastures of Gulf Coast Texas. It seemed like here in the dark we had been transported to Europe and were standing at the gates of some large castle inhabited by Count Dracula and his army of vampires. The castle was also surrounded by some of the largest trees in Santa Fe. The trees were giant oaks that were probably planted by the Karankawa Indians during the prehistoric times of the region. I pretended to be an Indian brave on a raiding party as we crept closer to the big castle. I imagined we would raid the castle and take home our spoils to the tribe. In my imagination I could see myself carrying jewels and gold back home to my Indian princess. I could see Rae in a deerskin loincloth and her long hair was braided with eagle feathers. Her legs looked beautiful in the moccasins made from deer-hide and rabbit fur. Rae always smiled at me in my imaginary thoughts. In the real world I thought she rarely smiled. My thoughts of Rae were interrupted rudely as Kenny reached back and shoved me down as a light switched on in the castle.

All three of us bent down below the tall weeds and stared at the upper window on the second story of the old castle. The light stayed on for a few minutes and then switched off. The castle was engulfed in darkness once again and we stood up. Terry decided we were close enough to watch out for the ghost so we spread down all the tall grasses and weeds and made a campsite. Our camp looked more like a giant bird nest and we couldn't have a campfire so we all reclined on the broken weeds. We watched the castle and the courtyard on the west side of the big walls. We talked quietly and ate our munchies for about an hour. Terry talked about a girl in Hitchcock that he liked. He said her name was Hilda. She sounded more like a witch than a girl but I didn't say that. I didn't want to hurt his feelings. He bragged about how pretty she was and how her body was awesome. We only believed about half of the stories we told each other anyway. Terry laughed quietly as he said, "Hilda is so dang fine! I was with her last week in the back of her Mom's car. We parked behind the school and I gave her about three hickies. She is a wild kisser."

Kenny said, "Okay we believe you, but how come I ain't never seen her in Santa Fe?"

"She doesn't come over here 'cuz her Mom won't let her. She told her that Santa Fe is just a bunch of rednecks and hillbillys and she don't want her daughter associating with them."

"I saw her at a basketball game in Hitchcock. She was hanging out with a blonde headed cheerleader named Randi."

"Yeah Randi hangs out with her a lot. You want to meet Randi? She has a boyfriend but he's a loser."

I said, "Hey, Kenny, go for it! You can kick his butt! Randi is probably hot too! Hitchcock girls are always wilder than Santa Fe girls!"

Terry punched Kenny in the arm and said, "Yeah, Bulbear, that Randi's got a rack. It looks like she stole two balls from the bowling alley and hid them in her shirt!"

We all busted out laughing at that. All the talk of girls and Hilda and Randi turned my thoughts to Rae. My thoughts seemed to always return to Rae. She had some kind of mysterious hold on my hormones or my brain or something. Maybe I thought Hilda was a witch but Rae seemed to have witch powers without even trying.

Terry suddenly put a lone finger to his lips to quiet everyone. "Shhh...I heard something."

All of our eyes stared at the shadowy courtyard, where Terry pointed. A shape moved across the courtyard. I just knew it was the ghost that Richard Chunbartio had told me about. This was the ghost that ate the heads of dead goats killed by Mexicans. This was the same ghost that howled at the full moon like a terrible wolf. This was the ghost that snuck into the rooms of the castle and played the piano, closed closet doors and opened windows in the winter. The shape moved eerily across the courtyard, almost floating in the darkness, and seemed to move the lawn chairs without touching them. We heard the chairs scraping on the cement patio. Terry crawled closer through the tall grass and we kept our eyes glued to the courtyard. A few minutes passed and the shape was gone. We heard a door close quietly. Suddenly Terry started hollering and jumped up like he was having a seizure or something. "Yaaah! Ouch, ouch, Ahhh!"

He began slapping himself with both hands all over his legs and thighs. Kenny and I just watched him like he was crazy. He screamed, "Ants! I got ants biting the crap out of me! Ants!"

He was trying to get the ants off as a beam of light shot out from the castle. Kenny and I still bent down low but Terry continued to jump and holler like an idiot jackrabbit. The bright flashlight beam landed on him. We saw a big man holding the light. He began walking out towards us. Terry stopped jumping and just stared at the light coming towards him. I could see the man as he neared and he carried a shotgun in his other hand. That was enough for me. I jumped up like a startled quail and took off running for the road with Kenny behind me. We heard the man yell, "Hey! Who's out there? Come back here!"

We ran hard and fast as only the terrified can run. While I ran I don't even remember how my feet or legs moved across the stickers and weeds. I felt like this is how the Flash must feel when he uses his super speed in his bright red spandex super-hero suit. I thought maybe I needed little lightning bolts on my head like the Flash. I reached my bike first and was pedaling away before the others. I never heard the shotgun go off so I guess Terry didn't get shot at behind me. I heard the man shouting again but I knew Kenny pedaled behind me. I glanced back once and saw Terry mounting his bike and start pedaling too. We rode for miles, down twisting and turning streets, to make sure the man with the shotgun couldn't find us. My heart was beating faster than an opossum trapped in the hen house with my Dad's flashlight shining in his eyes.

We stopped on Shouse Road, about mile from home. We were scared but now we all acted tough like it was more fun than scary. Now we could brag about the castle ghost to our friends. I never forgot those nights we camped out and the wild night wind in my face as I rode my bike speeding down deserted blacktop roads in Santa Fe. I never forgot Santa Fe nights, the way it was then, not like it is now. I never forgot the way I could see Rae out in the pasture, with the breeze in her hair as she read books I never heard of. The ghost castle campout was a favorite story and it grew in legend as we retold it at school many times.

"...THE TALL GRASS HID ME FROM THEIR VIEW."

Billy lived one street over and was a pimple-faced kid with white skin. His only interest was the band, KISS. Sometimes he would just be riding down the street on his old bike wearing KISS makeup, white and black paint on his face, usually to resemble Peter Criss the Cat-faced drummer of the band. I had heard from some younger kids that lived next door to Billy that they had seen Rae at his house. I didn't believe them at first so I tried to find out for myself. Why I should even care was weird but it seemed to trouble me at the time. One afternoon, after school, I followed Rae, without her knowing. I climbed on top of our barn and watched her cross the pastures towards Billy's house. I finally climbed off the barn and crawled low in the tall grass, trying to stay out of sight. I was close enough to see her knock on Billy's door, but the tall grass hid me from their view.

Billy came outside wearing a black KISS T-shirt and bellbottom jeans with holes in the knees. His frizzy hair was reddish and yellow and covered his ears and neck. At least he wasn't wearing his KISS makeup. Rae was talking to him and he came outside closing the door behind him. They walked over to the mimosa tree in his front yard and sat down, still talking. I couldn't hear what they were saying but I could see that Billy was eyeing Rae, dressed in very short cut-off blue-jean shorts and a buttoned shirt tied off just below her breasts.

Billy reached out and touched her hair and grinned stupidly and then he stood up and went back into the house. Rae just sat there and waited. He came back out of the house and was carrying something. Rae stood up and dug her tiny hand into her front pocket, pulling out a wad of money. She counted some bills out and handed them to Billy who smiled and handed her a plastic bag. I knew, even though I couldn't see very well, that she had just bought some weed. I was angry and upset and pounded my fist into the soft dirt. It wasn't my business, spying on drug deals or pretty girls but Rae seemed so magical and above this sort of behavior. Wasn't she too smart to be involved with this kind of thing? There was really nothing I could do. I started to turn around and sneak back home when I heard her shout.

I looked back and saw Billy grabbing at her and holding her hair with one hand. He seemed to be trying to force her to kiss him and at the same time trying to grab at her breasts. He pulled her to the ground and got on top of her, pinning her arms with his hands. Rae was screaming for him to stop and I ran towards them as fast as I could. Billy was taller than I was but I didn't care because he was hurting Rae. I jumped through the air, hurtling my body like a missile at his exposed back. My shoulders crashed into his ribs and backbone and his head jerked back at the impact. The force of my attack knocked his body off of Rae and we rolled through the grass. I clawed at his face trying to free myself from his grabbing hands. Adrenaline pumped through my body and I felt stronger than I really was. I placed both of my hands, which were filled with the power of rescuing Rae, at Billy's skinny throat. His fists tried to hit my back and shoulders but I squeezed harder and harder until his eyes began to bulge and he started to choke, gasping for small amounts of air, like a catfish left on the river bank.

He stopped hitting me and I could see the panic in his round eyes. I watched his eyes as they searched mine for sympathy and I could even see the little red veins in the white part as they wiggled like broken twigs on a rotten branch. Billy was afraid that he would die and I felt his fear seeping into my skin, a weird crawling sensation that pulled the strength from my squeezing fingers. I still held on and said, almost growling like an animal, "If you ever touch Rae again, I'll kill you. You get it?"

With his eyes bugging out like a squashed cicada, he nodded his head "yes" and I slowly released my hold on him. I stood up and he choked as he tried to stand. As I pulled away from him I looked at him, standing there, choking and trying to act so pitiful and it made me angry all over again. I quickly punched him in the stomach as hard as I could. He never even saw it coming and he fell to his knees on the ground. I glanced back at the tree to check on Rae but she was gone. She must have run home as we fought. Billy was crying and gasping for air and I said, "I mean it, Billy. Stay away from Rae."

Running to Rae's house I thought about how frightened she must have been. When I knocked on her door I kept thinking about Billy and of how he had tried to rape her. Mrs. Kimmings answered the door. She was taller than me but very thin with yellow and gray hair cut very short around her sea-shell ears. "Could I talk to Rae, please?" I asked trying to breathe normally. Mrs. Kimmings smiled at me and said, "Rae is not here. She left to go walking about an hour ago, I think. Maybe you could come back later?"

"Okay. I'll come visit her later. Thank you." I started to walk towards my house and then I turned to say "good-bye" when Mr. Kimmings walked out of the garage.

He shouted at me with a big smile on his face, "Hey, it's

my neighborhood buddy. Hey, tonight I'm going snapping turtle fishing. You want to come along and help me?"

"Sure," I quickly replied and continued, "Let me run home and ask my parents. I'll be right back."

I ran home still thinking about Rae and worrying about where she could have run off. My mom said it was okay to go with Mr. Kimmings so I changed into some old overalls and a T-shirt. I put my oldest sneakers on and donned my Astros baseball cap.

The canal was not very far from our street and we arrived there about a little before dusk. The roads back here were dirt and we stirred up a dust cloud by the time we parked next to the rise of earth covered with blackberry vines filled with little stickers. The canals were surrounded by hills overgrown with these sticker vines and all kinds of other weeds and clumps of brush, great for hiding snakes and nutria rats. Once I ran into a group of nutria rats and almost got knocked into the water of the canal as they tried to run over me to get to the water. These rats are closer in relation to the beaver than to a regular rat. They even look like a beaver, with two big yellow-orange teeth in the front popping out like tusks, except their tails are thin like a regular rat's. They live in and out of the water and seem to get as big as twenty pounds. I just try to stay out of their way.

When I was just a little kid my PawPaw, my Mom's father, told me a story about the wild Nutria rats that lived in the Chocolate Bayou. I was only about six or seven years old and had never seen a Nutria rat before and he told me this story the first time I ever went on a fishing trip with him. I remember that he always said that he would take me on a shrimping trip out on the ocean when he went but for some reason he never did. Even today I still think about all the times he asked if I wanted to go on a shrimping trip and I guess back then I was afraid to go. I think back and wish I would have went on one of those shrimping trips before my PawPaw died. I still miss him, even if my little brother was his favorite.

We went fishing at a bait camp that had piers out on the Chocolate Bayou, just Paw Paw and I. I was watching my cork, daydreaming about a giant green and silver alligator gar grabbing my bait, when I heard a loud splash across the bayou, near the shore. I saw a big circle of ripples and thought that maybe a big alligator jumped in the water. The loud splash startled me and my Paw Paw laughed and took a drink of his quart bottle of beer. He said, "Did you see that?"

He was still laughing, looking like a fisherman out of a Norman Rockwell painting, with his old baseball cap on his sun-burned head with a few hooks stuck in the front of it. I shook my head and said, "What was that, Paw Paw?"

He stopped laughing and got very serious, "That was a herd of Coypu Nutria rats all stampeding into the bayou. Them rats is as big as an alligator. Coypu rats came over here to Texas from some country in South America, somewhere like Brazil or Peru or Patagonia. They live in the Amazon River and even Piranha fish don't attack them. Their only enemies are big alligators and people. Some of the Indians in the jungles over there hunt them with poison darts and eat their meat but it is poison to Americans. Some American hunter captured some Coypu rats and brought them to Texas and released them into the rice canals. He told people that they would control the weed problem in the rice fields by eating all the problem growths. The giant Coypu Nutria rats just loved it over here because there wasn't as many big gators and there wasn't any poison darts flying at them. Them rats just kind of took over the canals and the bayous. Hell, they even live in the ditches behind some of the neighborhoods in the cities."

My eyes were getting bigger as he told me about the giant rats and I asked, "Paw Paw, how come the Piranha fish didn't even try to eat the rats? I seen a show on television about those fish and they can turn anything into a skeleton in about a second with their sharp teeth."

My Paw Paw tilted his baseball cap back on his forehead and squinted in the sun reflecting off the water of Chocolate Bayou and replied, "Nutria rats have big fangs hanging out of their mouths like saber-tooth tigers. A wild herd of Nutria rats can spot a school of piranha fish and stampede into the water, slashing and biting, eating the fish before they even can attack the herd. Nutria rats are vicious animals and very dangerous. Never get in the water with them. I heard an old crabber tell a story about how a little boy fell in the bayou out of his boat and he landed in the water next to a momma Nutria rat and her babies. Well, she squalled and the entire herd of them big rats came running into the water and swimming at the boy. The old crabber said that you could hear them fangs slashing in the water. Before the boy's father could reach out in the water from the boat them rats had already got to him and started attacking and then they just dragged him underwater. After that happened a bounty was put out for killing Nutria rats and they were hunted down and skinned for years but it never even put a dent in their population. Coypu Nutria rats are just too smart and tricky for people and they can stay underwater for a long time. Even the entrances to their tunnels are underwater, like beaver's den."

I was scared back then and I barely asked, "Did the boy ever get found?"

"They found parts of his body all up and down the bayou but they never found his head. The old crabber said the boy's head was probably up in some Nutria rat's den."

"Paw Paw, you ever seen a Nutria rat attack somebody?"

"Naw, but I did see a bunch of Nutria rats come after an old dog that was swimming in the water. The dog and the rats were fighting in the water and the next thing I knew was the dog went underwater for a long time. Finally the dog came up but I didn't see any Nutria rats. The old dog swam to shore and he was limping but he was okay. Maybe he killed the big rat, I don't know, but he never liked to go in the water much after that fight."

I found out later that the Nutria rat, *Myocastor Coypus,* was introduced into the Gulf of Mexico in the 1930's. Nutrias are larger than muskrats but smaller than beavers, weighing about sixteen pounds. They were marketed as the next "mink" and at one point a breeding pair sold for $2,500.00. The Nutria fur trade never caught on but the Nutria rat loved America. They multiplied in the marsh and swamplands. In 1938, Tabasco millionaire, E. A. McIlhenny brought the Nutria rats into his Avery Island Park and by 1957 there were 1,000,000 Nutria rats in Louisiana. The Nutria rat ranges all the way up in the east-coast states now, and is blamed for vegetation destruction and erosion of the landscape in marsh areas.

My Paw Paw liked to tell me stories while he drank his quart of beer and stayed outside in the Texas humidity. He never went very far without that quart of Falstaff beer. He used to sneak us sips of beer when we were just little kids. I didn't like it but I thought it was great that I could drink a beer like a man. My Paw Paw even had a square wooden beer bottle holder built into his old white Plymouth station wagon. The laws were different back then. I guess if he were alive today he would be arrested for an open beer container in his car.

I will always remember his glasses and his baseball cap and that quart bottle of Falstaff beer. He almost always had one ear plugged up with the radio speaker because he loved baseball. He used to take my brother and I to the Houston Astros baseball games in the Houston Astrodome. These trips seemed to take days to complete because he drove about forty-five miles per hour the entire way there. The Houston Astrodome is only about forty-five minutes away from Santa Fe but it probably took us two hours to get there. At least that's what it seemed like. My Paw Paw was an interesting man but I don't remember everything that well. I remember his stories and his views but not really what his heart said inside.

We got the tackle box from the back of the truck and I carried it while Mr. Kimmings carried the lines filled with hooks and a bucket of chicken meat to be used as bait. Mr. Kimmings turned to me as we stood on top of the hill overlooking the long narrow body of water. I was looking back into the setting sun and could only see his silhouette and I remember how large he was, like a giant of the earth blocking out the light, claiming the night as his prowling time. I could see one edge of his profile and his long, curly handle-bar mustache caught a shiny gem of light from the receding sun. He said, in a quiet voice, "I'll set my marker and secure the lines if you bait the hooks with the chicken."

"Okay." I replied in almost a whisper. I was taught by my father a long time ago to be quiet when you are fishing to keep from scaring the fish away. I didn't know if snapping turtles could hear us talking up here above the canal but Mr. Kimmings was keeping his voice low so I followed his example. We stretched lines all up and down the canal for about hundred yards and then we headed home. On the way back Mr. Kimmings began talking to me. "Later, we'll come back and reap our harvest. I'll bet we're going to have plenty of big turtles and catfish to eat after this trip. Oh, by the way do you mind if I ask you a personal question?"

I didn't so I just nodded and he asked me with his big smile momentarily gone, "What do you think about Rae? I mean is she getting along with the other kids around here? You've lived here all your life, how do you think she's fitting in? I'm concerned about her. She seems to be by herself a lot."

"Well, I think she has some friends. She is really nice, I mean, I like her. She's very pretty."

He laughed and replied, "She gets that from her mom. She is a pretty girl. Do me a favor and help her adjust. She probably could use a friend like you."

I didn't know what to say, so I just said, "Okay."

When we got home Rae was sitting on the front porch in the hanging swing, reading under the porch light. Mr. Kimmings turned off the truck and said to me, "She reads a lot…go talk to her."

I jumped out of the truck and walked slowly towards the porch, observing Rae as I approached. I heard Mr. Kimmings go in the house through the garage and we were alone. I could see the curl of her thick lashes as her downcast eyes were shadowed by the overhead porch-light. Rae's tan legs were crossed at the ankles and her hair was tied back with a white ribbon. She was just a frightened girl in a new place but to me she was a goddess. She was a supernatural mystique of great beauty that froze me and kept me from approaching any closer. The blood that flowed within me had become solid and I had trouble breathing. I thought about how it must feel to be a hooked snapping turtle under the water, trapped on a barbed piece of metal, unable to swim to the surface for air. A big prehistoric, scaly snapping turtle twisting beneath the water on a hook trying desperately to rise above the surface for sweet oxygen. I was so nervous and afraid. She had not even looked up from her book. I could hear the calling of cicadas in the trees and the occasional squawk of an erratically flying nighthawk. Looking out into the darkness of her yard I saw a few fireflies winking their little lights like lost floating stars or the tiny fire of life that I had seen within Rae's eyes as she finally looked up from her book.

Her facial expression was unreadable but she kept looking at me. I said, "Hi, Rae. It's a nice night."

She said, "I should be mad at you for today but I have to thank you for helping me out. Billy was my only connection to buy what I needed and now you've ruined that for me. I'll be black-balled from buying the stuff. But thank you for stopping him. Each time I came to him to buy he would get a little bolder and try things. Up until today I had been able to control him. If you hadn't been there I think…I…oh, I don't know what could have happened. I mean I heard he did things to Leslie but she more than likely let him. I'm just glad you were there. Thank you again."

I could have been mistaken but I thought that I saw a tear streak down her cheek and my inner core started to melt like a slow cracking glacier inching down the jagged rocks of a mountain. I wanted to hug her, to hold her and tell her that I would have killed him if he ever hurt her. I wanted to shout at her and tell her I would protect her and help her and always be there for her. In that moment I think I fell in love for the first time. I walked over to her not really comprehending what I was feeling but reaching out to her with compassion. I sat down beside Rae and put my arm around her. She hugged me back and whispered, "Thank you."

She stood up and touched my cheek with her fingers and went inside her house. I sat there awhile until the porch-light went off and then walked home, my feet about an inch above the ground.

"TURTLES, CATFISH, CARP, AN OCCASIONAL GAR, AND SOMETIMES SNAKES,"

I didn't see Rae for quite awhile after that night even though I watched for her. I found out later that she went to stay with one of her aunts in West Virginia for a few weeks. I had been going with Mr. Kimmings regularly to the canal and catching catfish and snapping turtles for the fish fry. Mr. Kimmings always called me "Buddy" and I kind of liked that. My Dad would've taken me fishing but he worked all over the country, a week here and a week there, working construction jobs. Sometimes he did take me fishing and we caught a few bass and bluegill sunfish and every once in awhile we caught bullhead catfish but I always liked to go and pull up those lines in the canal with Mr. Kimmings. The exciting part was watching the bait come up and never knowing what was going to be caught on those big hooks. Turtles, catfish, carp, an occasional gar, and sometimes snakes, poisonous "Cottonmouth" water moccasins, black on top with white scales on their belly, would be hooked on the line. Every time I went with Mr. Kimmings I would hope to just catch a glimpse of Rae at her house before we left or after we got home. One time I remember she was looking out of her bedroom curtain as we pulled out of the driveway. Our eyes met in the slowly dwindling light of dusk. She was staring at me with a longing from a far away place, like I was a tropical island that beckoned her to shed her sadness and pain. It was as if I called to her to lie on white sandy beaches to watch the blue-green surf roll gently in. Our eyes held one another's for only seconds as the truck backed out of the driveway and then I saw the curtain slowly close and the tips of her fingers slipped from the window. Mr. Kimmings was talking to me about snapping turtles and treble hooks but I could only see her fingers slipping out of sight. That window of glass shadowed by cloth covered the soul of Rae and draped a veil of mystery over whatever separated her from my world.

The Kimmings big neighborhood fish fry was held on the Fourth of July and even people from a few of the other streets near our street were invited. It started about noon and people started showing up in the Kimmings front yard. Mr. Kimmings had erected a big tent on poles that he borrowed from his church to shade the old people and the babies. A few of the other men in the neighborhood, including my Dad, were helping with the frying of the fish but most of the men were drinking beer and sitting in lawn chairs under the shade trees. I was over by the front fence under the big oak tree watching some of the teenage boys playing horseshoes. Mr. Kimmings house, like the other houses in Santa Fe, was built on a couple of acres of property and his front yard was about a whole acre, plenty of room for the fifty or sixty people who had shown up for the fish fry.

Mr. Kimmings had turned up the stereo he had in his garage and country music blared out into the yard. I heard songs by Johnny Cash, Merle Haggard, Tom T. Hall, Loretta Lynn, and Dolly Parton. Over by the fence, where I was, the teenagers had backed Billy's friend Joe's old pickup truck in the ditch and placed his homemade speakers on top of the cab, blasting rock music trying to drown out the old people's country music. The speakers kept vibrating and fell off the truck twice.

Standing by the fence at the fish fry in the Kimmings front yard I watched the games of horseshoes. I listened to the clang of the metal horseshoes as they struck one another and the spike sticking up from the ground. I watched the games but I was thinking of Rae. She hadn't emerged from the house yet. She must be inside helping the women get all the rest of the food prepared. I just couldn't picture her cooking or preparing food. The image of Rae actually doing such things didn't exist in my observations of her. More than likely she was in her room reading poetry or meditating to some of the nature gods in reverence of the dead snapping turtles spirits, guiding them into the arms of the Dominions of Mother Earth.

I watched a kid throw a ringer, the horseshoe clanging as it struck the spike and slid down embracing the shaft of the spike with the curved "U" of metal. The image was unsettling. The shape of a dead snapping turtle's shell curved with a big knife impaling the middle of the turtle. I felt chills spread up my arms and back and looked up. Rae was only ten feet from me. She came forward with a bowl of food and a glass of punch. Her blonde hair was streaming out behind her and blinding me with the image of silk spun from the shiny spiders of the golden sun. My stomach fluttered and I struggled with words, managing, "Hi, Rae."

She smiled. Her smile came from somewhere inside those secret depths where she kept all her treasured things. Her smile that she extended to me was a gift. The wrapping paper flew from around her and all I could see was that smile. "Hi, I brought you the first tastes of the food because you helped Dad catch everything."

She handed me the bowl and the glass of punch and

turned and walked deliberately back into the house. I looked around and all the guys playing horseshoes had stopped and watched her walk away. When she closed the door behind her they turned their eyes to me. I looked down at the ground and slowly chewed on a piece of fried catfish. The horseshoes began clanging again and I walked away to the big oak tree on the corner of the Kimmings yard. I sat down to eat the food Rae had brought me. I'm sure some of the fried meat was snapping turtle but I didn't even distinguish the difference at the time, my thoughts on the strangeness and the mystery of Rae.

After all the food was served to everyone, the older men started telling stories, which were really exaggerated lies, and most of the younger people snickered and ribbed each other in the background. After the beer began to flow more freely and the stories died down to whispered dirty jokes, Mr. Frinton, the old hermit/widower from around the corner, stepped into the crowd of people in the Kimmings front yard and cleared his throat. Everyone stopped and turned their attention to him because Mr. Frinton hardly ever spoke to anyone, much less to a crowd.

Mr. Frinton lived in a little pink wooden house in a tree filled yard with a narrow gravel driveway. He hardly ever came outside but somehow his yard was always kept immaculate, the lawn mowed and edged. Near the road at the front of his lawn he had the biggest tree in the neighborhood, a huge, ancient Ash tree. I still remember when I was about ten or eleven years old, I had tried to climb the giant tree. Somehow I had gotten about twenty feet off the ground in the monstrous branches and I heard my Mom calling me to come home and eat supper. I had been just sitting in the tree, dangling my legs over the branch, swinging my tennis shoes back and forth amazed at how the sky didn't seem any closer even though I was high up.

I decided I had time to climb higher in the tree before I ran home for supper. The decision was one of the worst decisions in my entire life. I climbed easily up the huge branches and could even see the roof of my house across the pasture behind Mr. Frinton's house. I was admiring my climbing ability, imagining that I was clad in a lion cloth and I had become Tarzan of the Apes, searching the ground for my enemy, Numa the lion. At that moment something big flew by my face and startled me. I almost lost my grip and fell backwards but I held on, feelings that chill of fear and adrenaline rush through my body like ice-water. Suddenly I felt a stab of intense and excruciating pain at my left temple. I screamed as I felt more bolts of violent pain on my back and my chest. Large things were flying around me and at me. I flailed my free hand wildly, somehow coherent enough through the awful pain to maintain my grip on the branch. I saw one of the black and red hornet's stab into the back of my hand and I let go of the branch, yelling like a banshee as I fell backwards. I only fell a little ways, landing on another branch and I didn't even feel the scrape of the rough bark on my skin as the swarm of hornets punished my flesh with their vicious stings. I climbed, crying and screaming in terror, down out of the tree as the hornets pursued me. I jumped the last few feet to the ground and started rolling on the ground. Tears covered my stinging face and I scrambled to my feet and burst into a sprint towards my house, screaming, "Momma! Help me! Momma!"

I never climbed that tree again. No one in our neighborhood would even get near that tree after seeing my swollen face and body. The other kids took one look at my big red puffy ears and cheeks and swore that the Devil had attacked me with his pitchfork.

As I looked at Mr. Frinton, remembering the hornet

attack in his front yard, I waited for him to speak, curious about the strange old guy. Mr. Frinton was in his seventies or eighties, maybe even ninety, at least he looked that old with a zillion wrinkles all over his face and arms. He wore overalls and converse tennis shoes and he was never without his straw cowboy hat. He cleared his throat with a sound that resembled a cough hybrid sneeze/fart. That sound alone was enough to get everyone's attention. He raised his right hand and spoke. "I just wanted to say, "thank you" for invitin' me to this big feed. I would also like 'un to tell you folks a tale of these parts afore many of you 'un got to livin' out here."

I searched the crowd as Mr. Frinton spoke, watching everyone, searching for those beautiful eyes of hers. Searching for Rae. She was sitting up against a Chinaberry tree, almost isolated and detached from the bulk of the people. She held a book in her hands and marked her place with her finger as her eyes followed Mr. Frinton. The space across the crowd of people seemed to shimmer, almost like the effect of a mirage of water on a hot road and I felt my skin tingle. Rae eyes met mine in that instant. It was as if I could see a new world, a different zone of awareness channeling out to me in that moment. I tried to blink but she held my eyes open with her stare. My stomach grew cold and I felt trickles of sweat dropping from my forehead. I gazed into her and swam on a dizzy sea, tossed on a surreal liquid vision of mountains made of clover and flowers. I could see glacial ice and caverns with molten centers. I watched creatures of unidentifiable form and shape leap, crawl, and stride on open savannas, vast plains of tall grass and oddly distorted cacti. I flowed into giant lakes and merged in that instant somewhere I had never been. I panicked and sucked in a deep breath, filling my lungs with air and squeezing my eyes shut. I could hear Mr. Frinton speaking as if from the depths of a deep well. I kept my eyes shut and continued to breath and finally my body began to return to normal. I stopped sweating and my breathing slowed. I opened my eyes again and looked at Rae. She was reading her book and twirling one long strand of her hair with her fingers. I tried to look away from Rae's face but I could only stare like a possessed fool.

I could hear Mr. Frinton continue with his story. He was saying in his gruff voice, "When I was just a bean sprout we used to have a fish fry in the county park. Brazoria County was still a dry county back then but we use to smuggle in the liquor and the beer. Heck we used to even make our own beer. All the men in the county would bring their best catch to the park and the women would cover the picnic tables with colorful tablecloths. Sometimes I had seen one hundred and fifty-pound channel catfish brought to the fish fry. The one time I do remember most is the story I want to share with ya'll today. I was a teenager then and following my nose after the girls who came to the fish fry. I expect there was one hunerd or more people there not counting people's kin from outa town. We were all sitting under some big oak trees talking to the girls and watching squirrels dash among the branches. I had my eye on a girl for some time and her name was Louise, Louise Wentzle. I would have probably married her but for what happened at the fish fry that year.

My two friends, Joe Anderson and Lindale Maird, were talking to Debbie and Dottie, the Templeton twins and Louis and I were chit chatting 'bout the squirrels playing in the tree-tops. Joe was a fast wiry guy and a good athlete and Lindale was big and clumsy but strong as a Brahmer bull. I remember all of these things clearly. Outa the corner of my eye I saw him coming. I saw him walking like he was king of the town. He was strutting like everyone should bow before him. I grimaced at his approach and elbowed Joe to look around. Joe and Lindale's happy smiles disappeared replaced by frowns. All our conversation stopped as we awaited his approach. He was followed by two of his cohorts.

His name was Kevin Gawk and his pals were Sneaky Stevens and Roger Pitts. Kevin was in his twenties but only smart as a 'lil kid. He worked as a mechanic and his fingers were always black from grease and oil. He was the biggest guy in Brazoria County, standing over six feet five and weighing bout as much as a wrestler. His teeth were crooked and ugly like his twisted smile. Kevin had been in and outa jail and had broken Deputy Haid's nose with his large elbow. He hung out at the Little Seadog Bar over by the railroad tracks. A place decent folk always avoided."

Mr. Frinton poised here to sneeze, "A-choo!"

And the crowd murmured a chorus of "Bless you."

He wiped his nose with a magically appearing handkerchief and started speaking again without a hitch, "They say Kevin Gawk killed a foreigner in the Little Seadog Bar with a billiard ball but no one ever proved it. Fact is, they found the foreigner's corpse a week later bout a mile down the railroad tracks. His body had been run over by a train."

I was starting to get interested in the old man's story and everyone else was quiet, intently listening to Mr. Frinton slowly spin his tale. A few of the men watched the fish cooking as the story spun a hypnotic web and I watched Rae twirl silk hair on her fingers. Rae seemed to be listening but her eyes switched from her book to Mr. Frinton and back and forth. It was like watching a blue strobe light flash on and off, her eyes glowing and then flickering with those long delicate lashes.

Mr. Frinton paused for effect and scratched his fat ear, continuing, "Draw your own conclusions but most folk believe he killed the foreigner, and the train did not. The reason Kevin had been in jail mostly was cuz he got drunk and got in fights. The Sheriff department didn't like arresting him unless they had to cuz his cousin was a State Representative. I only know that Kevin Gawk was an evil and despicable man without any goodness in his soul. Sneaky Stevens and Roger Pitts fit right in with his crazy company. Sneaky got his name honestly from an old Gym Coach we used to have, Dodger MacDonald, who caught Sneaky stealing from the boy's lockers at school. Since that day in sixth grade everyone called him Sneaky because of Dodger MacDonald's paddling him in the Gym Office with the Board of Truth. Dodger's paddle was called the Board of Truth. He called it that because he could get the truth outa any boy by using it on them. That paddle was 'feared' and it kept many boys from ever acting up. The Board of Truth was five feet long and solid oak, with holes drilled into it for air-flow. Sneaky lasted three wallops with the Board of Truth before he screamed his truth. That boy was crying for hours after that paddling.

Sneaky quit school in ninth grade and got a job in the hay fields and then later with the county of Brazoria, mowing grass on a tractor. Sneaky later got married and had some kids but his wife divorced him and moved to Vermont. They found Sneaky dead on his tractor on New Year's day. Both of his hands were still gripping the steering wheel. He had vomit running down his front and the tractor was outa gas with the key still 'on.' Sneaky died of alcohol poisoning at the age of thirty-six.

Roger Pitts made Sneaky look like a preacher-boy. Roger was a gambler, whore chaser, bully and all-around criminal. He had only been outa prison for 3 weeks when he showed up at the fish fry with Kevin and Sneaky. I never knew what happened to Roger after all these years but I heard he went to prison again and then got parole. All three of those hoodlums were stone skunk drunk. Roger Pitts was chewing on a flavored toothpick, he always had wads of them in his pockets, and Sneaky puffed on a cigarette with the ashes long and curly like a brittle squid's tentacle. As they approached, Kevin starting being his usual obnoxious self and said, "Well, well if it ain't a bunch of love birds sitting under the tree. What ch'all doin' under the tree stealing little hen peck kisses?" The girls just looked at him with disgust and me, Joe, and Lindale all stood together expecting trouble. We always expected trouble when Kevin Gawk was around. We stared at him hard with our fists clenched and our jaws tight. I saw the vein in Joe's forehead start to throb. That always happened when he got riled up. The three hoodlums stopped a few feet from us and they stared right back at us. We were younger than them but we weren't afraid. Roger spit his toothpick out at us and it fell to the ground next to my boot. Sneaky shuffled his feet and he flicked his cigarette away as he stood, feet spread apart like a soldier at ease. Kevin was smiling, showing his uneven teeth, and he laughed at us, saying, "Wow! Ya'll look like real tough guys to me. Sittin' here under this big old shade tree with a bunch of girls watching squirrels up in the branches."

About that time a squirrel accidentally dropped an acorn from the tree above Kevin. The acorn fell and bounced off of Kevin's greasy hair and then dropped to the ground. I saw him look up at the squirrel with utter hatred and he quickly grabbed his hair. The acorn didn't hurt him, he was just startled and embarrassed. I couldn't help myself and busted out laughing. Joe and Lindale also bellowed loud laughs at his funny misfortune. The squirrels rustled in the branches above and the girls all started giggling. Sneaky and Roger stared at

Kevin expecting him to tell then how to act. Kevin started turning red like a tomato face and I knew he felt humiliated by the squirrels and our laughter. We couldn't stop laughing at him though. I wish now that we had. Kevin Gawk was a criminal and his rage had consequences. We never could have dreamed what would have happened next.

Kevin reached behind his back and un-tucked a pistol from his shirt and jeans. He started screaming, "Just shut up! Just shut up, now!"

He pointed the gun at the squirrels in the trees. The little squirrels just looked at him like he was harmless. They didn't have a clue about Kevin Gawk. I actually thought the squirrels thought his actions were amusing as they watched him with tiny dark eyes glittering down from the branches. Kevin started shooting at them.

The squirrels dove behind branches and dodged behind limbs. We all jumped for the ground, including even Sneaky and Roger hitting the dirt. Kevin stood there firing into the tree when suddenly Louise was upon him.

I remember her eyes that day. When I had been talking to her I could see deep into her. Her eyes were like laughter and lust and I lived in them for those moments. Louise had a sweet, syrupy laugh and it sounded like wind chimes. She was a life path and I thought about her road. The way her hair curled up on the ends and the way she snapped her fingers quietly when she was thinking. I remember her eyes when she launched herself at Kevin Gawk. They were the eyes of fire and fearlessness. The light shone in them intensely. Her face seemed calm in the storm of her eyes and body as she grabbed the gun in Kevin's hand. Kevin jerked back from her pulling the trigger one more time as squirrels scattered from sight. Kevin didn't kill one single squirrel.

Louise had her left hand on Kevin's gun and her right hand on his neck as she stood there facing him. Kevin stood still looking into the face of Louise Wentzle. I saw her nostrils flare and her eyes flicker as she looked down at the scarlet stain on her blouse. A wisp of smoke drifted between them from the barrel of the gun. Her eyes started to look over at me but before I could see the light from them, Louise's eyes closed. Her knees buckled and she fell to the ground. Kevin let her fall and his face turned pale as if the light from her eyes had shone too brightly and bleached his skin. He looked at us once and I saw fear in him. He turned and ran with Sneaky and Roger on his heels. All the people in the county park had heard the gun shots and were quiet as the three boys ran away from us. We were silent and stunned. I finally blinked and ran to Louise on the ground. Debbie and Dottie were kneeling beside me. I turned Louise over and her eyes were closed. I remember seeing her thick eyelashes curling upwards. She was like a sleeping beauty. I yelled, "Get help! Somebody please help!"

A crowd of people suddenly surrounded us. Their quiet voices of shock and curiosity filled the shadows under the big tree. I held Louise's hand and the back of her head off the ground. I didn't want dirt to get in her hair. I didn't cry. I felt numb. The hate of Kevin came later as did the sadness of loosing a special woman in her youth. Louise saved the squirrels and went to Heaven with an Angel's escort.

Lindale suddenly shouted, "Kevin Gawk did it! The murderer! We all saw him kill her! Kevin Gawk shot her!"

Everyone stared at Lindale as he screamed, demanding that lightning or thunder would validate our loss. Finally Dr. Withers came and pulled my hand from hers and I was led away by Debbie and Dottie. The police came and broke up the crowd. Debbie and Dottie never screamed or went into hysterics. They cried rivers of tears in the soft moaning sadness of shock. They both clung to me like Selly Mo bee honey. I remember tasting a tear that trickled down into my mouth. That taste of salt filled my reservoir of pain.

That fish fry at the county park taught me love and hate in the same day. I still go out there and touch the place where the bullets cut into the big tree. I go there on quiet summer days and watch the squirrels play in the branches."

Mr. Frinton just sat down in a lawn chair with his head in his hands. Everyone stood looking at him as if they expected him to just melt into a puddle of tears. He looked up then, above the people and into the trees. I followed his gaze, as did everyone, including Rae. I saw tears in her eyes as she watched Mr. Frinton searching the tops of the trees. I figured he searched for Louise in the sky, gazing down from Heaven. Then I saw what he looked for. A fat squirrel was watching him, clinging to the tree and blinking its eyes. One more blink of those little black eyes and it disappeared, scampering like a rustling ghost in the leaves and branches.

Rae continued to stare at the treetop long after everyone stopped. People returned to their games and tasks of preparing the food but a somber mood had slipped over the fish fry. People thought of their own losses and heartaches. I watched Rae's eyes stare upward looking like polished rocks. She was calm and serene with tear tracks glistening on her smooth face. Her hair whipped back from her face and a few unruly strands waved like stranded wheat plants in a cow pasture. She suddenly glanced away from the tree and looked directly at me. Those wet eyes were solid and powerful and saw emotion roiling in her soul. She held my gaze for only a minute but I reached out to her with my eyes. Rae wiped her tears with the back of her hand and walked quickly to the picnic tables where her father stood.

I enjoyed the food of the fish fry and watched Rae move about the tables serving people. My dad and mom were sitting by the Kimmings. They were all laughing and eating fried shrimp while Mr. Kimmings was explaining how to catch a tub full of snapping turtles. The snapping turtle soup was cooked in a large tub over a big flame, which sort of looked like a campfire. Other people were eating blue crab and fried flounder while sipping bowls of snapping turtle soup. I liked catching snapping turtles but I was afraid to eat the turtle soup so I ate plenty of fried shrimp and French fries. After most of the people finished eating all the wonderful seafood the somber mood improved. The atmosphere grew boisterous as the day wore on and dusk approached.

"I SEARCHED THE SKY FOR THE SIGNS OF THE FIRST BATS,"

The sun diminished behind the tallow trees and night birds chirped behind the hedges. I scanned the sky for the signs of the first bats, flying erratically snapping up insects in flight. The south Texas dusk is a beautiful scene. The horizon glows with a pink and orange sheen. A pastel blue then fades into a slowly growing gray sky. The tallow and the pecan trees turn into black silhouettes like skeletal giants from a dark planet. The wind whispers through the tall pine trees and sings scary lyrics of the coming night.

The miniscule little bats, *Tadarida brasiliensis*, also called Mexican free-tailed bats, zipped through the darkening gray of dusk like miniature stealth bombers. The Mexican free-tailed bats live in colonies under bridges, in caves, the eaves of houses and even in palm trees. Some of the world's largest Mexican free-tailed bat colonies are only about a three-hour drive from Santa Fe, in the capitol of Texas, Austin. The Mexican free-tailed bats are the same species that inhabit the famous Carlsbad Caverns in New Mexico.

I used to ride my bike to the edge of the old deserted nursery, which in the summer is like a lost, out of place, tropical jungle, and wait for the coming of dusk. I would stand up on my bike and marvel as the light slipped slowly out of the world and the gray rolled in. Squinting my eyes in the almost darkness, I watched in amazement as the bats began to appear. Darting about in the air, like minnows avoiding a bass, they snatched tiny insects from the air. Those were magical times, alone on that dirt road with a dark scary jungle to the south and black shadows with winged membranes zooming and zipping above my head. Sometimes the bats would fly very close to my face almost as if they wanted to get a closer look at this strange thing that observed their flights at suppertime. I have never caught a bat but I once found a dead one in a swimming pool. I guess it had a crash landing in the water and drowned. It wasn't a Mexican free-tailed bat but one of the Red bats that looked like little cute Pomeranian puppies in the face. I remember feeling sad as I fished the wet fur winged creature from the pool.

The people at the party did not look up into the darkening skies in search of a glimpse of the Mexican free-tailed bats as I did but instead drank more beer and munched on the few remaining fried shrimp. My mom was helping clean up, as were most of the women. Rae was pulling the turtle tub out to the backyard. I got up and went to help her. She smiled and said, "Thanks."

Her voice was almost a whisper. I glanced again at the sky hoping for a glimpse of the tiny bats and then grabbed the other handle of the big tub. We carried it out back and dumped the remaining broth out in the cornfield. I carried the tub behind the house to the garden hose. She turned on the water and began cleaning the tub . I didn't get out of the way soon enough and she sprayed me with the water hose. I shouted, laughing, "Hey! Watch it, girl!"

She laughed like a mockingbird singing in spring. It thrilled me deep inside to hear that laughter. Rae started to point the water hose at me again and I ran to get out of the way of the spray. She continued to laugh at me and said, between giggles, "Water won't hurt you. C'mere and get cleaned off. You need a shower anyway!"

"Stop it now, I don't want to get wet. Okay?" I said this laughingly, just happy to be flirting with her. This was the most I had ever seen Rae act silly. She just wasn't a very playful person. This side of her surprised me and made the serious girl I knew even more mysterious. I remember that evening behind the house, with the moon creeping across the near-night sky. The shadowy cornfield was behind us as the wind brushed the corn stalks creating a sound like armadillos applauding our playful show. Rae's hair reminded me of the golden silk of the cornfield as the breeze fingered separate strands about her neck and shoulders. Her blue eyes became violet in the dusk and I could see the moon reflected in them.

She stopped spraying me with the water and, still giggling, started to clean out the turtle tub. I just stood there by the corn stalks, which were taller than I was, and watched her. My trance was broken when Rae's friend Jade stepped around the corner of the house. She walked towards us with her heavy-footed stride and her jeans made a friction sound as her large thighs rubbed together. Jade opened her big mouth and ruined the atmosphere immediately, saying, "Hey Rae! You want to go with a bunch of us over to Galveston and hang out on the Seawall?"

Rae glanced at me, and then replied, "Yeah I want to, but what are we going to tell my dad?"

Jade made a goofy face and burst out with her harsh laughter and said, "Silly girl! I'll tell him you're spending the night over at my house with the girls. Leslie told her mom the same thing and my parents are out of town. We'll go to Galveston and then head back and have the house all to ourselves."

Jade looked at me and said, "Why are you hanging around here anyway?"

I just shrugged my shoulders and mumbled, "See you later Rae."

I walked back around to the front of the house where the rest of the people still sat around telling lies and stories and drinking more and more beer, determined not to let any go to waste. I felt lonely and sad because of the way Rae always seemed to not even have any clue how I feel about her. I was older than she was but I felt like I wasn't hip enough or cool enough to understand her crowd. I would never be accepted in her crowd and she would never understand what was important to me. She was like a star, a twinkling little star in a violet sky. Rae was a tiny star in a vastness that was filled with many clusters of large stars and constellations. She didn't fit in any of the galaxy. She was off all by herself in a corner of the universe, twinkling where only I could see her.

It was dark now and the yard lights were on and a few torches were lit. The mosquitoes were starting to bite and swarm and old lady Marhing was going around to the leftover children and spraying them all over with insect repellent. I hated the insect repellent as much as the children did. They would close their eyes tightly and scrunch all up as she sprayed that stinky stuff all over their arms and legs. One kid, my cousin, Kenny Bulbear, would run from her. She could never catch him and he would hide until the can of spray was empty. He was always covered with sores from scratching his many mosquito bites. The can wasn't empty yet and all the kids had been sprayed except Kenny. I saw him hiding up in the Chinaberry tree in the front yard. Old lady Marhing saw him too and hollered at him to come down before the mosquitoes carried him off. Kenneth just sat up there without any intentions of moving.

I saw him constantly slapping mosquitoes away though. Old lady Marhing finally gave up and went inside to put the spray up. As soon as she left, Kenneth jumped from the tree and ran down the road in the dark. I couldn't see them, but I knew little bats dodged his running head as he ran into the dark.

"I LOVED WALKING IN COW PASTURES."

The next day I opened my eyes early and decided I needed to get out and walk. My thoughts were not on Rae this morning but on adventure. I would go across the cow pastures that separated my friend Matt's house from our road. The two cow pastures I walked in were about a mile wide. I loved walking in cow pastures. There were few trees, except for small Chinese Tallow trees with bent, twisted limbs. I would sometimes find wild patches of sticker vines filled with blackberries. At least once a summer my mom would give us old empty coffee cans and we would go out in the pastures in search of blackberries. My mom would make blackberry pie and blackberry cobbler. I have heard that in other parts of Texas people call blackberries by another name. I guess some people call them dewberries, but here I have only called them blackberries. I remember I used to always want the blue coffee cans as opposed to the red coffee cans. I don't remember what brand of coffee it was, I think maybe Maxwell House or Folger's, but it didn't matter, I didn't like coffee anyway. My cousins and my brothers and sister would get our cans from the garage and set out on a berry picking expedition.

The last thing my mom would say is, "Watch out for snakes!"

I would watch out for them because I wanted to catch every snake I could. I loved catching snakes. The blackberry vines were covered in tiny stickers. The vines didn't grow very tall, only bout a foot or two above the ground and tangled into all kinds of other weeds and stickers. One day I found a giant patch of blackberry vines and began picking them only to start hollering immediately. The blackberry vines were growing in a large patch of stinging grass. Stinging grass looks like faded clover and invisible little needles stick in your skin when you brush against it. Stinging grass is more painful than fire ant stings. I would always run for the water faucet and get cold water on the sting. This method never worked but at least I felt like it did. I think that rabbit in the Tar baby story ran into a blackberry sticker patch to escape that red fox, but I don't think there was any stinging grass in there. Even rabbits don't like stinging grass. Blackberry patches always had a glob of white spit on the leaves and some older kids had told me that this white stuff was snake spit. I never found out if this was true or not. I always found it disappointing to gather blackberries and not run into any snakes. Most of the kids were out there to see who could find the most berries but I was out there to find snakes, the berries were just an excuse. Everyone would fight over the biggest and best berries when a new cluster was found but my little sister, who was one of the youngest and didn't know any, better, would always end up with half a can of red berries. The red berries were blackberries that were not yet ripe. Truth is I really didn't like blackberry pie very much but I liked going out there in the weeds and stickers.

Rae once gathered berries with me on a warm spring day. I will never forget how the breeze touched the back of my neck and I imagined it was Rae's golden hair tickling my skin and her soft lips kissing my neck. We both laughed so much that day as we raced to beat each other in grabbing the biggest juiciest blackberries off the sticker vines. That day was one of the times I felt close to her; almost close enough to feel like I understood her. Rae didn't worry about snakes at all. I think Rae wasn't afraid of any wild animals. She seemed drawn to all animals. Once I even saw Rae let a huge skeleton-back yellow garden spider crawl on her hand and up her arm. She let that big creepy thing crawl up in her hair sit on top of her head. I think that was the scariest thing I have ever seen anyone do. I hate spiders tremendously and that is one creature I have no reason to touch. It shocked me that she would have no fear of spiders. I once walked full into a large garden spider web and freaked out, jumping like a madman and flailing my arms to rid myself of the webs on my face and neck. I stopped flailing and stood still, searching the ground for the crawling big spider when suddenly I felt it under my shirt in the back. I screamed and ripped my shirt off quickly, like it was on fire. The spider was tangled in my shirt and I threw it in the bayou. Losing my shirt was worth losing that big spider with it. I was deathly afraid of the spiders but snakes didn't scare me, or Rae. She had this invisible aura or something magical that maybe only animals could see. I have seen her get closer to wild animals than anyone else could. It seemed as if wild animals trusted her. To this day I don't know what she did or what she possessed but wild animals acted strangely around Rae. I thought I must have been a wild animal too, because I always seemed to never be able to act like myself around Rae either. I had never seen her catch a snake but I have seen her near them and they don't slither away quickly like when I'm after them. I once saw her approach a ribbon snake and, I swear, the reptile crawled closer to her bare feet and flicked its tongue out touching her toes. That was the weirdest thing I have ever seen. Rae wouldn't let me catch the snake but made me let it crawl slowly away into the sticker bushes at the side of the road.

I was a snake catcher from the time I got brave enough

to grab one behind the neck. I caught all kinds of snakes and wished there were more varieties in southern Texas for me to discover but it isn't a big snake paradise. I always dreamed of catching something more exciting like an anaconda or a python. The most dangerous snake in our part of the world is the western cottonmouth water moccasin, *Agkistrodon piscivorus leucostoma,* and we have plenty of those. All water snakes in this part of the country aren't poisonous but cottonmouth water moccasins are highly venomous. The problem with water moccasins is that they are almost identical in markings and size to other non-poisonous water snakes. Water snakes are aggressive and bite viciously but water moccasins possess two fangs in the roof of their white mouth that inject a toxic poison. Cottonmouth water moccasin's are also related to the deadly copperhead. Both snakes are in the venomous Pit viper family. I have always noticed a strange behavior when encountering a cottonmouth water moccasin. The snake, when agitated, acts like it is a rattlesnake by vibrating the tip of its tail. It is called a cottonmouth because when angered it opens its mouth wide to reveal the snowy white inside of its mouth. Water moccasins are everywhere there is water. They are semi-aquatic and feed on everything from frogs, fish, salamanders, other snakes, birds, mice, even baby alligators.

Most water moccasins are about four to five feet in length. They are fat heavy snakes but they are extremely quick. A cottonmouth water moccasin is even dangerous when it is dead. Once I cut a moccasin snake's head off and the decapitated head still tried to bite. Once I was fishing with my dad at a far away lake. We had caught some large mouth bass and a few bluegill when my dad said, "Hey come over here, I think I got something big."

I ran over to him, dropping my pole on the ground, and

watched him reel in his fighting catch. It was a big crappie, maybe a two-pounder. We didn't catch many crappie, large perch-like fish, in these small ponds. I saw the fish fight right up to the shore when suddenly a loud splash of water exploded by the fish. A large black water moccasin struck from out of the dark water and bit into the struggling fish. The fat snake gripped the flipping fish in its mouth and twisted its slippery sinuous body around the fish. My dad reeled the fish in, with the big snake coiling and squirming, attached to the crappie. My dad yelled at me, "Stay back! Go get me the machete' from the truck!"

I ran back to the truck and got the machete' from behind the seat. My dad put down his fishing pole well away from the water and took the machete from me. He said, "well we can't eat this fish now, it has damn snake poison in it."

I said, "but dad why can't we eat the snake? I have a friend at school and he said they eat rattlesnake all the time. His Grampa catches them in Bandera and they cook up snake steaks."

My dad kind of laughed and replied, "Look son, nobody but a crazy person would want to eat a fat stinky water moccasin, with poison for blood."

He took the machete' and chopped quickly down on the snake's head. The headless snake body writhed like an out of control octopus tentacle. My dad picked up the writhing long black snake and tossed it far out in the pond, saying, "This is some good gator food."

He took his pocketknife out of his pocket and cut his fishing line. "Well," he said, "looks like I lost a good hook with this crappie and snake head."

He chopped the head a few more times for good measure and to make sure the head would stop biting. He stabbed the fish with the machete' and tossed the dead fish and snake's head out into the water. My dad smiled at me and said, "We never can have enough dead moccasins. My uncle Lance stepped in a nest of water moccasins while hunting wild pigs. Those snakes bit him so many times, so fast, he almost didn't have time to scream. I wasn't born yet but my aunt told me the story. My uncle Lance died from those damn water moccasins. I kill every poisonous snake I come across and you should too."

Fishing that day wasn't the same after that. I kept thinking that a giant black serpent with white fangs would attack every fish I would reel in. I caught many snakes during those years but I always killed cottonmouth water moccasins. I often wondered what kind of snake put their spit on blackberry vines but I didn't think it was water moccasins. Billy over on the next street called it frog spit and said that only rabid leopard frogs spit on the blackberry vines. I never saw a frog spit but I did see Billy always spitting like he chewed tobacco even though he didn't. Billy did have one thing in common with leopard frogs though; he could burp as loud as they could croak. I couldn't even count how many times he got in trouble in school for burping obnoxiously in class.

Today I wasn't worried about water moccasins because I wasn't near any water. I was crossing the cow pastures to Matt's house. My mom told me to watch out for rattlesnakes but I had never seen a rattler in the area. My mom was a paranoid snake worrier freak. I think all mom's are. I did keep an eye out for coral snakes when I stepped through cow pastures. Coral snakes are very poisonous too. They are red, yellow, and black banded and are related to the dangerous African cobra. Coral snakes are not Pit vipers like copperheads and moccasins. There is another tri-colored banded snake that looks like the coral snake but isn't poisonous. It is the Louisiana Milk snake. There are many varieties of king snake that resemble the coral snake but only the Louisiana Milk snake has the same black snout, most imitators have red snouts. The Louisiana Milk snake's red bands touch their black bands while the old saying, "red and yellow, kill a fellow, " fits the color pattern of the deadly coral snake. I wasn't too worried about coral snakes though because I had only killed one in all my years.

I did think that it would be great to catch a Louisiana Milk snake though and bring it back to the house to show Rae. I think she would realize it was a beautiful snake. I didn't know if she liked snakes or not but she seemed to like all animals. I had a baby opossum before and she really loved it. I liked it too but then it got out and our dogs killed it. She used to like my hamsters too but the cat got them.

I walked across the pasture looking under pieces of wood and rocks for Louisiana Milk snakes or something just as unique to impress Rae. I took my time crossing the pasture because I liked exploring. I would sometimes be very still when I saw a bird nearby and see how slowly I could approach it. Sometimes I got very close before they noticed me and flew away. Certain birds let you get closer than others. Meadowlarks did not let you get very close but mockingbirds and killdeer would let you walk right up on them. Mockingbirds didn't care because they were brave or maybe they had the knowledge that they are the Texas state bird and it is against the law to kill them. Killdeer, a banded plover, a shorebird that doesn't reside very near water, are loud little birds. Their cry sounds like their name, "killdeer, killdeer."

The reason they let you get close to them is simple, they have an alternate plan in mind. These smart little birds fake having an injured wing to lead you away from their nest. When they get you to follow them and you get too close they just fly farther away. They then laugh about it, having fooled you, and gotten you away from their nest. I used to try to sneak up on them in the schoolyards but I finally figured out what they were doing and gave up.

I walked across the dry grass of the pasture, following the barbed wire fence line that ran down the middle of the two pastures. I saw some cows ahead and watched the African cattle egrets, cowbirds, follow the big cows around darting their beaks after the bugs that turned up around cattle. The African cattle egret is a cousin of the snowy egret, a long necked white marsh bird with long legs and beak for grasping prey. I noticed a big white bull near the cows and their calves at about the same time as he noticed me. He snorted and stomped his hoof into the dirt. The big bull had a massive hump on his back. I knew he was probably a Brahman cross of some kind. He started a slow charge at me and I didn't panic because I knew I could escape easily by crawling through the strands of the wire fence and getting safely on the other side. As the big bull charged I could hear his heavy hooves throwing dirt up behind him. He bellowed and gathered speed as I climbed through the wire. He pulled up short at the fence, saliva slobbering from his mouth. I stood well away from the barbwire and watched him warily as he stared at me. I was safe unless he decided that he could tear the fence down. I figured he didn't want to trample me that badly and I began to walk across the pasture again. A few steps away from the bull is when I noticed that there were cows on this side of the fence too. I turned away from the bull on the other side of the barbwire and discovered I was in more trouble than I had thought.

I saw a huge angry Santa Gertrudis bull trotting towards me. The big red bull made the ground thunder as he built up speed. I ran for the fence, seeking escape, but the big white bull on the other side blocked my exit. I was trapped between the two large bulls intent on charging and trampling me between them. With a bull on either side of the fence I had to search quickly for another avenue of escape. I sprinted down the fence line with two bulls charging and bellowing behind me, getting closer. I felt at any moment I would be tossed high in the air by the giant red bull. He would catch me on his big head and toss me to the other side of the fence where the white bull would impale me on his curving horns. I was scared to death as I ran. My bare feet didn't even feel the stickers or the thorns that stuck me as I ran. I saw a lone tallow tree standing in the pasture and broke away from the fence line, sprinting for the tree, I hoped I could get there and climb high enough to get away from "big red" before he smashed me into the ground. I reached the tree only seconds before the big red bull and I leapt up in the branches like Tarzan of the Apes. I heard the bull pass underneath as I continued to climb higher. My heart was beating like a snare drum in a military march. I was safe from the big red bull. He stood on the ground beneath the tree, patiently waiting for me to come down. I waited and waited and the bull refused to leave. He kept glancing up into the tree at me as if he expected me to actually come down and take my medicine. Well, I knew he was in for a long wait. I had no intentions of coming down and facing that huge animal. I thought he would get bored or tired and finally leave. I waited and then I thought maybe I might be up here awhile when I saw that all the cows and calves were gathering around the bull beneath my tree. I looked around the pasture hoping that suddenly the rancher that owned these pastures would show up. I could see Elroy Brannon's house about three hundred yards away, the closest house to these cow pastures. Elroy's kids went to the junior high but I knew them and I had talked to Elroy a few times at the bus stop down the road. I remember one time I helped him catch his raggedy dog, Fancy, a collie-mix, when it got loose. I sat staring at Elroy's house for about half an hour when suddenly I sat up straight in the tree when I saw Elroy come out his back door. He went into his storage shed behind his house. I was ready to shout at him when he came out of the shed but I heard his tractor start up. Elroy came out of the shed riding his tractor. I knew he wouldn't hear me shout over the roar of the tractor's motor. If I could have looked in the mirror at that moment I would have seen a big frown on my face. I was disappointed and frustrated at having to be trapped in this tree because of a bunch of stupid cows and a stubborn bull.

I imagined myself as Tarzan and I could see myself jumping down on the bull's broad back. I would plunge my sharp knife into the bull as he bucked and tried to kill me. I would hold on to one horn and stab with my free hand until the bull would collapse. I would stand with one foot on the dead beast and holler to the world of my triumphant victory over the mighty bull. My mom would probably beat me when I got home because of all the blood stains on my blue jean shorts. I guess maybe being Tarzan wasn't such a good daydream.

I watched Elroy riding his tractor and wished he would look this way. He was a bald skinny little man and he always wore a railroad cap, with blue and white pinstripes. I saw his dog, Fancy, running around on his rope barking at mockingbirds in the backyard. Fancy was a pretty stupid dog. Smart dogs never paid any attention to mockingbirds or any birds at all, except quail or doves and that was only because they were taught to hunt them. I thought that maybe Fancy was raised by cats and that would explain his peculiar obsession with mockingbirds. Mockingbirds seem to be very vicious when a cat is in the area. Once I saw a cat walking very slowly across a lawn and a mockingbird furiously attacked it. The bird must have dived at that cat at least twenty times. The cat only walked slower and ducked each time he felt a swooping attack coming on. If I was that cat I would have suddenly leapt up and spun around, claws outstretched and grabbed that "pain in the butt" bird right out of the air. Finally the cat disappeared into a row of thick hedges and the bird flew up on the mailbox. Sitting on the mailbox, the mockingbird flexed its wings out two or three times and made clicking noises, proclaiming victory over the cat. I can still see that gray and white bird sitting on top of the mailbox, flexing those gray wings and opening its beak shrilly announcing bird gibberish to the sunny day. I looked back at Elroy's house and two mockingbirds flew up on top of his house chattering and landing on the television antennae.

Elroy rode that tractor like a man possessed, his skinny body bouncing up and down with each bump in the ground. Suddenly I heard a loud crack. Elroy's tractor abruptly stopped. I saw him stand up, shaking his head and slapping his thigh. He must have run over something and broke his tractor. I immediately started shouting at him, "Hey! Hey! Help! Mr. Brannon! Help!"

Elroy heard me and stopped looking at his broken tractor and looked in my direction. I was standing on the branch and waving my arms, shouting, "Hey there! Help!"

He began walking in my direction and I saw him crawl between the barbed wire fence strands. He picked up a long stick and strode towards the tree. I glanced down at the cows and the huge bull beneath me. The bull saw Elroy and pawed the ground, snorting. The cows milled around nervously. I started yelling at the cows, "Go on! Get out of here!"

The bull was about to charge and Elroy swished his stick and yelled at the big red bull, "Shoo! Get away bull!"

I jumped up and down on the branch and yelled at the bull too, until the branch I was on snapped and broke. I fell so fast I hardly remember even being in the air. I landed on the bulls back with a thump and bounced up towards his head. I saw his eyes rolling wildly to see what had gotten on his back. I tried to hang on but I fell off as he jumped up and kicked out with his feet. The bull bellowed and twisted in the air as I fell on the dirt and sparse grass. Elroy shouted at the bull and ran over towards us. The bull didn't want any part of me any more. My fall and crash landing on his back had startled and spooked him. He trotted away from the tree with the entire herd upset and briskly running behind him. Elroy helped me up from the ground and asked, "Are you okay?"

I thought I was, but my butt and back felt differently. I was only bruised and shook up but I said, "Sure, I'm not hurt. Thanks for the help."

I wasn't hurt except that I found out later that Rae had seen me fall out of the tree. She had been out walking, picking up different pebbles that she sometimes collected and glued onto pieces of wood. She wrote poetry and pasted it on plywood and then shellacked it and glued all kinds of things around it like rocks, shells, feathers, and other things from nature that she discovered on her many walks. I could have made up some great story about how I tried to ride the bull and got bucked off but Rae had been there and witnessed my accident. My plans for a good story of bull riding were gone now that she had been there.

"RAE HAD PRETTY LITTLE FEET..."

It was a few days later when I was down at the end of the road, watching minnows in the ditch that Rae approached me unexpectedly. I was so engrossed in watching the darting little fish that I never heard her until she stood right next to where I sat in the shell dust at the edge of the road. She stood next to me and I noticed she was wearing those straw thongs and her toenails were painted red. Rae had pretty little feet and her toes had tiny blonde hair on them. I thought those little blonde hairs were the cutest thing but I would never tell anybody that. She said softly, in that haunting voice so different from everyone else, "I saw you fall out of the tree. You could have been hurt. Do you feel okay?"

Her presence startled me and I always seemed to have trouble speaking my true feelings but I replied, "Uh, yeah, I just kinda' hurt my back and my ribs a little but I'm okay, really."

She put her hand on my shoulder and bent down, saying, "That bull almost killed you. A few inches closer and you could have been trampled to death. It's a good thing Mr. Brannon was there. He frightened the whole heard of cows away."

Rae sat down beside me in the shell dust. Our dead end street used to be topped with oyster shells instead of the blacktop that covered it now and the edges of the road always accumulated the crushed dust of the shells. It was like a soft white powder. I liked shell dust because it made nice false smoke like a miniature hand grenade when you filled a cup and threw it. Shell dust swirled like a tornado when the weather acted weird and dust devils gathered it up and spun down our short road. Dust devils made of shell dust are almost like living animals. Dust devils are when the wind gathers granules or objects like paper or dirt and spin them in a circular motion similar to a tornado. I always wanted to capture a dust devil and keep it in a room with glass walls so I could watch it from time to time. I scooped some shell dust up from the road in my hand and held it up, saying to Rae, "This is what a dust devil is made of, shell dust and wind. The wind comes from somewhere far away and finds the shell dust waiting. The wind talks to the shell dust in a mysterious voice and the shell dust is pulled along by some earthly magic. The wind and the dust are joined together in a dance of a peculiar rhythm above the ground. The wind curls around the dust like the embrace of some lost lover and they swirl into the air. The wind hugs the dust tighter and tighter, forming the twisting little tornado of shell dust and wind."

Rae stared at me. Her eyes looked different and her face held an expression I had never before seen. Rae was quiet and her mouth was slightly open, with her lips parted. I almost thought she looked like she would kiss me. She swallowed and blinked her eyes but continued to stare at me, saying, "That is the most beautiful thing I have ever heard."

I could hear her breathing and the world seemed to get very quiet at that moment. I was silent for a few seconds and just listened to her breathing, in and out. I wanted to kiss her but I was afraid. She half-closed her eyes and leaned closer to me. My heart hammered inside of my chest. She kissed my cheek and I sat there in some sort of trance. Rae smiled shyly, and whispered, "You are different than I thought. I never knew you had thoughts like that going on inside of your mind. Why do you always pretend to be Mr. Country-boy when you have the secrets of the arts inside? You are just afraid to become what your destiny tells you. I guess it is because of Santa Fe. This town molds you into a life that does not include the many facets of the world. This place has borders and boundaries that you aren't even aware of. I can see how people like it though. Some of the borders are good for life here. You will never fulfill your destiny if you stay here forever. Remember my words. The butterfly flutters from flower to flower exploring the world and the slug spends its entire life in one garden. You could become the rare butterfly. I know I don't want to be the slug staying in the same garden my whole life."

I didn't know what to say. I just sat there and listened to the most words she had ever said in a row. She had just kissed me on my cheek . My cheek still felt damp from the moist pressure of her pretty lips. I tossed a pebble into the water and watched the tiny minnows scatter. The ripples from the pebble reminded me of the rings of Saturn. I thought about what she had said. It was beautiful too, the story of the butterfly and the slug, what a comparison.

I wanted to become a butterfly but how could that happen? I knew that this was my home. I liked it here. Everything was familiar and safe. I loved the tranquility of the open pastures and the shade of tallow trees. We sat there watching the minnows and I felt so emotionally close to Rae, almost as if we were truly a couple. I knew this was only my fantasy, Rae would not be thinking the same thing. I think if we didn't live on the same dead-end street in cow town Texas we would never even talk to one another. I grew up in this town that has roads ending with gates and cattle guards: (the steel pipes across the open gate that allows vehicles to cross but cattle cannot walk across the pipes without falling in between them and breaking their legs). Santa Fe has the same families doing the same things, generation after generation. If Joe Bob Shyler owned the Feed Store then Joe Bob Jr. would own it next and after that Joe Bob the third got it after that, and so on. The same law applied for the Drug Store and the Grocery store, the Barber Shop and the Twenty Four Hour Café.

Rae wasn't born here so she didn't understand this strange way of life that had outlasted the world. I thought everything ended here and began here. I wouldn't find out until much later that the rest of the world has different rules. Rae didn't like the idea of killing snapping turtles for soup. The snapping turtles in Rae's mind became a symbol of strength and freedom and the hooks that caught them like regulations that imprisoned the people. When her dad, Mr. Kimmings, took the snapping turtles from the water it made her think it was like trapping people into places with walls and corners. Dead snapping turtles were the image of a death trap for Rae. She knew that she needed to escape from this small town someday. I understood her viewpoint but I never got past the fear of what lies beyond the borders of Santa Fe.

I tossed another pebble into the water, I was aiming for a striped green crawfish but missed, and the pebble plopped with a tiny splash. I grinned and said, "missed the crawdad."

Rae squinted from the sunlight and smiled a half-smile. She reached over and touched my face. I was surprised and didn't quite know how to react. She extended her right hand and found my hand. Rae traced my fingers with her fingers and the sensations I felt were indescribable. I was mesmerized. My heart was beating like the flapping gills on a stranded fish on the pond bank. She stopped abruptly and her fingers interlaced with mine. She held my hand gently. My thoughts whirled and

I realized with full incredulity that we were holding hands. I was holding hands with this mysterious, enchanting girl, Rae Kimmings.

Rae and I sat there for about a half hour talking quietly and enjoying the sensation of being close to one another. I didn't want to ever stop holding her hand or looking at her face so close to mine. She finally said, breaking the spell, "It's getting late. I better head home because I have a lot of things to do this evening."

She let go of my hand and I felt something inside of me slip away. That was not a pleasant feeling. I looked at the water and noticed that the striped green crawfish had returned and I also knew it was time to go home. I looked into Rae's eyes and said, "Yes, I guess I better get home too. My mom probably has been looking for me. Thanks for sitting with me and talking."

Rae stood up and brushed off her legs and I got up too. We stood there feeling awkward and uncertain. I longed to kiss her and knew that this was the best time I would ever get. She seemed to look expectantly towards me and we leaned together. I was about to kiss Rae when we both saw Terry walking towards us with a broken tree branch swishing in the air like a sword. "Hey ya'll! Catching crawdeads?"

That was it. The moment had passed and I felt like a rainbow had lit up the horizon and disappeared before I could even see it. I stepped one step away from Rae and she did the same. I yelled, "Nope, just throwing rocks at minnows. We were just getting ready to go home. Where are you going?"

Terry looked at us sort of funny, like we didn't look the same to him or something, and said, "Uh, well, I was just walking and saw ya'll down here and thought maybe ya'll wanted to stay out until dark and watch for bull bats or nighthawks."

Rae said, "Well ya'll can but I need to get home. See ya'll later."

She walked away, leaving Terry and I standing by the minnow ditch. We both watched her walk down the road until we saw her turn into her yard and disappear from our sight behind the oleander bushes. I picked up a rock and threw it hard into the water, making a big loud splash. I saw the muddy bottom stir up and the crawfish shot backwards with powerful flips of his tail through the murky water. Terry swished his long stick in the air making sounds like flying gulls. I watched the ripples from the rock and thought about kissing Rae Kimmings, the wonderful girl who thought honeybees were her friends.

"I THOUGHT OF MYSELF AS THE PLANET MERCURY, LITTLE AND INSIGNIFICANT,"

I didn't see Rae for weeks after that day. I was playing football in the pasture with the other guys in the neighborhood or hiking or searching for animals to capture and bring back to put in jars or cages. Rae was either hibernating in her house with her books or out running the roads with her weird friends. We just never ran in the same circles. I would climb on the roof of the barn at night and lie on my back, watching the stars. I thought of myself as the planet Mercury, little and insignificant, rotating around in the solar system like a solitary atom in the vast universe. I imagined Rae more like the planet Saturn, the most unique planet with those vapor rings around it, unlike all the other planets that circle the sun. Rae and I existed in the same world but we were moving in our individual circles that hardly ever crossed paths. If only I were a moon held by gravity or magic close to the planet Saturn, within the protection and comfort of the encircling rings, I think I would feel closer to the sun's rays without the burning heat of isolation.

Sitting on the barn roof one night is when I finally saw Rae again. I was sitting on the rusted tin listening to the zooming sounds of diving nighthawks when I saw Rae walking towards the pastures behind our houses. I could see her long blonde hair shimmering in the moonlight like an albino ermine perched atop her head. I watched her walk slowly through the tall grass. She was wearing a sheer night-shirt and shorts. Rae stepped underneath the barbed wire fence carefully and continued out into the pasture. She never saw me sitting on top of the barn. She was carrying something in her right hand and she stepped cautiously because she was barefoot. Although we had plenty of snakes around it seemed Rae never thought about encountering one. Watching her move surreally through the pasture like that seemed so dream-like. I felt like she wasn't really there, like I was watching a ghost twin of Rae glide through the pasture a few inches above the ground.

Every instance that I have seen Rae I have felt an unearthly feeling like nothing I have ever experienced to this day. I don't know what it was about her but I can still sense and remember that feeling somewhere deep inside of my soul. I glanced at the stars above and returned my eyes to watching this amazing, unique enigma of a girl glide through the tall grass of the pasture. Rae stopped about one hundred yards out in the pasture and sat down. She moved around a bit and then she stretched out and reclined in the grass. I could barely see her out there but I saw her take her shirt off. She put her shirt on the ground and she reclined on it. She was too far away for me to see anything except for her blonde hair but the thought that she was out there shirtless made me tremble. I was afraid to move or make a sound. I didn't want to disturb the moment or interrupt her in any way but I knew I had to get back in the house before my mom missed me. I was as still as a statue and that's when I saw a big opossum creepily walking along the barn roof towards me.

His little claws were slightly scraping on the tin. I actually thought the tiny sounds would reach Rae and she would discover me on top of the barn. Without fear of hurting myself I leapt off the roof onto the ground behind the barn. I landed hard and rolled directly into a sticker bush. I tried to untangle myself from the thorns without getting too scratched up but the pain of the thorns would not be as bad as the shame of being discovered on the barn by Rae. I finally got out of the sticker bushes and had only about ten scratches on my back and one on my neck. I glanced out into the pasture but the grass was too tall down on ground level and I couldn't see Rae anymore. I wanted to sneak out there and see her but I was too afraid. I went back to my house with the thought that Rae was out in the pasture without a shirt on. I couldn't stop my imagination from overworking and sleep came hard that night.

"...LIKE A BROKEN LEGGED JACKRABBIT ON HOT CEMENT."

The Indian Dance was approaching in less than a week. It was a community dance sponsored by the school and the local ranchers association. Everyone in town would be there. It was the second largest event besides the yearly County Fair and Rodeo. I was going to ask Rae Kimmings to go with me. I hadn't told anyone about my plans. I knew I had to act fast before one of those long-haired freaks she hung out with asked her before I did. Every time I thought about getting brave enough to ask her to the Indian Dance my heart would thump around like a broken legged jackrabbit on hot cement.

Jade Morgan and Leslie Gertone were hanging around the Buzzy Bee Trailer Park, sipping Jack Daniels whiskey from Styrofoam cups. They had skipped school and had been down in Galveston at Stewart Beach all day. They were both badly sunburned and had white raccoon eyes from their dark sunglasses. Sharleen Little had provided the girls with the whiskey and the cups. Leslie was wearing a confederate flag T-shirt and Jade wore a yellow tube top that barely contained her large breasts and belly roll. Jade was an easy target for some of the older men she had been with when she was drinking whiskey. Even though she was underage the bartender always let her into the Wagon Wheel Oasis, a run-down dump of a bar on Highway 6, because she had let him sleep with her many times. Jade had very little self-respect and not much more intelligence than any of the other local drunks. Jade knew she would never finish high school. Leslie could finish school if she wanted to but she only had a desire for hanging out and getting high. She didn't sleep around as much as Jade but she would let men have their way if she could get weed from them.

Sharleen Little was barely over thirty but she looked older. She was still pretty even though she had wrinkles around her eyes. Some people said that she used to be a Homecoming Queen back when she was in high school. When Sharleen frequented bars men always tried to pick up on her. She had an athletic body and she sometimes still went down to Runge Park to play tennis with her cousin, Pam. Sharleen worked at the Santa Fe Feed Store. She did the accounting and sold feed and fertilizer. Sharleen had worked there for at least five years and the owner, Jasper Cook's widow, Marci, thought highly of her abilities.

Jasper had died in an accident out in the fields with a hay bailer and left her alone with a good business but no life insurance. Marci was only twenty-seven years old. She wasn't a beauty queen but she had a cute smile with only one dimple on the right side of her mouth. Her red hair was the talk of the town. Young girls that went in the feed store with their fathers saw her red hair and wanted to dye their hair the same color. Marci appreciated Sharleen so much she had given her a Christmas bonus last year of five hundred dollars. Marci learned that Sharleen was a lesbian soon after she hired her.

Sharleen stayed away from the advances of men and didn't like their company after hours. Marci and Sharleen had been to the café after work on Friday nights and became close friends. One Friday night after eating at the café Sharleen had invited

Marci over for a drink. That night was a night with no moon and nighthawks swooped in the darkness like stray missiles without guidance systems. Marci and Sharleen had talked about high school memories and their early lives. Sharleen was from a small town up near the Big Thicket, Liberty, Texas. Marci had grown up in Santa Fe and her father had served many years on the school board. Sharleen made Margaritas and they both talked freely as they drank. The night passed quickly and both women were more than a little drunk when Sharleen touched Marci's face lightly with her hand, pushing Marci's red hair out of her eyes.

Marci giggled but Sharleen had a serious look in her eye as she said, "Marci, I like working down at the Feed store. I'm glad I work for you. I have been wanting to share something with you, but I don't want you to judge me or stop being my friend."

Marci stopped laughing and said, "Sharleen, you can tell me. I appreciate all the work you do for me. In fact, without you helping at the store I don't know if I would be doing so well."

Sharleen put her hand on Marci's cheek and bent forward and kissed her lightly on the lips. Marci didn't react. Sharleen pulled back and watched her reaction. Finally Sharleen said, quietly, "Marci, I'm a lesbian. I am attracted to you. If this bothers you that is okay and I will be just a great friend an employee to you. Marci I don't want to ruin our friendship. I only wanted you to know the truth behind my life. This is a small town and rumors abound. I try to keep to myself but Santa Fe is a hard place for me to live. You have given me an opportunity when I thought that I might not find one anywhere else. I just wanted to thank you for your friendship and generosity."

Marci was feeling the tequila in the Margaritas and it had been a long time since anyone had kissed her. Marci leaned forward and kissed Sharleen back. She kissed her a long time and then leaned back, sighing. Marci looked deep into Sharleen's eyes and said, "Thank you Sharleen. It has been forever since I have been touched or kissed. I'm not a lesbian and I still miss Jasper. He was my true love. I should be going now but this night will stay with me a long time. Friendship like this is hard to find. Thank you, again, Sharleen. See you Monday morning."

Marci left the trailer and drove home slowly, crying. She thought of Jasper sitting on the fence post holding her hand as they watched the setting sun over the rice fields of southern Texas. She remembered the way Jasper used to kiss her in the barn when they were dating. Sharleen had reminded her of Jasper in her friendship and her sweetness. Jasper would always be her true love and she couldn't conceive of anyone ever taking his place in her heart.

Jade and Leslie sipped their whiskey from the white cups leaning against the railings of the porch on Sharleen Little's trailer. Sharleen was inside watching television but her door was open and she kept an eye on the two girls. She knew she shouldn't give them liquor but they would just get it somewhere else and at least she could keep an eye on them. A blue Camaro pulled into the trailer park and rolled to a stop next to Leslie and Jade. Rory Marks was driving and Fred McGlocum was riding shotgun. The Camaro had a silver hood, bought cheap from Miller's Wrecker Yard. Rory shouted to the two girls, "Have ya'll seen Rae around?"

Leslie tossed her cigarette to the ground and walked around the car to Rory's side. She leaned in his window and said, slurring her words, "Rae ain't interested in you, boy. She ain't been around for weeks. Rae likes to keep to herself. You boys partying tonight?"

Rory looked at Fred and it was like they read each other's mind. Leslie and Jade were both drunk and easy. It was a slow night with nothing else to do. Fred called Jade over to the car. Jade took another sip of her Jack Daniels and leaned in his car window. Jade leaned and whispered, "Hey Fred, what you doing out here at the trailer park?"

Fred said, "What are you drinking Jade?"

"Jack Daniels."

"Mind if I have a sip?"

"Sure, Fred, go ahead."

Jade took a mouthful and then leaned in the car window, kissing Fred, and pushing the whiskey into his mouth with her tongue. Rory watched and then turned to Leslie, saying, "What are ya'll doing hanging out at the dyke's house? Sharleen Little trying to get in your panties?"

Leslie, smirked, "No, Rory, but she's all right. She gets us the liquor when we need it, that's all."

Rory laughed, "Whatever girls, get in and let's go for a long ride."

Fred got out and let Leslie get in the front seat, while he and Jade got in the rear. Sharleen watched as they pulled out of the trailer park. She shook her head and grimaced and turned off her television. Opening a new bottle of wine Sharleen ran herself a hot bath and soaked up her melancholy life with heat and bubbles.

"...I WOULD END UP LOOKING LIKE THE LEOPARD BOY."

The next day I saw Rae out in her front yard, sitting like she always did, Indian style, reading books. Her golden hair rode the slight breeze like a ghost tied in a tree on Halloween night. I was in my front yard sitting on a big rock in the rock garden my dad had created and the Mimosa tree shaded my back from the direct sunlight. I wondered if being partially shaded like this if my back would tan in spots and I would end up looking like the leopard boy. I watched Rae a little longer, building my courage up to cross the yard and sit beside her. The real bravery would come when I would get up enough nerve to ask her to the Indian Dance.

A blue jay screamed in the branches above me and I tried to see his bright blue feathers through all the leaves. I saw him when he decided to find another tree and flew into Rae's yard, landing in the tallow tree next to the fence. I stood up, following his lead, and walked across into Rae's yard. She was so engrossed in her book she never noticed me coming until I was standing right in front of her. I plopped down in the clover beside her and she looked at me like I was just a Mockingbird flitting by. She always puzzled me. One day I was close to her, the next she barely knew me and I barely knew her. I choked up and didn't say anything at first. I was already nervous about asking her to the dance and now I was extremely terrified. Rejection would be a hard blow to take at this point in my life.

Rae turned a page and looked up from her book, saying, "Hello, I'm reading selected poems from Percy Bysshe Shelley. I especially like "The Cloud." I keep reading it over and over again. I love the way her words are so beautiful describing only the clouds in the sky. She brings the clouds to life. They have personality and power, purpose and magic. Have you ever read "The Cloud?"

I was dumbstruck. I had never heard of Percy or "The Cloud" and certainly never thought of clouds having power or magic. I was thinking about asking her to the dance and now I wasn't so sure of anything. Most girls I knew would be talking about the dance or a new dress they bought or their cheerleading practice or the rabbits they were raising for the Galveston County Fair and Rodeo at Runge Park. Rae was still staring at me expecting an answer. I looked into her eyes and felt like I could see forever. I started to ask her right there to go to the Indian Dance with me but I stammered something else like, "Uh, "The Cloud?" I never did get to read that one. I once saw a dark cloud that came slowly from the northwest and the temperature dropped so fast your sweat dried on your skin. I remember that dark cloud started growing a funnel at the bottom of it and headed this way towards our house, almost like it was following our dead-end street sign. We all got out in the yard and watched it spit out lightning in all directions. Our cows started bellowing and ran into the barn. My dog whined and high tailed it to the garage. My dad came outside and yelled at us to get in the house. We started to run for the house when the funnel cloud got bigger and a loud noise like a train wreck filled the air. My dad hollered again, "It's a tornado! Get in this house, quick!"

All the kids turned and ran to their houses but I couldn't move. I just stood there like I was frozen or something. A crackling bolt of lightning hit the tree next to me and I could feel the heat and the electricity on my skin. The hair on my head, which wasn't much, was standing straight up. That ash tree broke apart like a cannon shell hit it. Suddenly I decided to stop being a frozen kid and ran like a cottontail rabbit into the garage. We all huddled in our house, crouching down in the den, staying away from the windows, even though I wanted to see what was going on. I just kept imagining that our house was going to get picked up by the tornado like Dorothy's house in The Wizard of Oz!"

I was talking nonstop and Rae was still looking at me. I think this was the most I had ever talked to her without stopping. I was nervous about asking her to the dance so I just couldn't close my trap. I rattled on like a weirdo car salesman on a television commercial.

She just stared at me with no expression and then said, "I was afraid of the witch in Oz. She had a mean green face. I don't know why but I liked the flying monkeys, though. I know they were supposed to be evil but I liked them and thought that they were cute. I think you are cute, too."

I nearly fell over in the clover. I know I couldn't have heard her correctly. Did she say I was cute? Or did she say I looked like a flying monkey? I gathered courage because I thought that maybe I had an opening and replied, "I liked the flying monkeys too! Rae, I have always thought you were cute, well, actually better than cute. I came over here today to ask you if...if you wouldn't mind...going to the Indian Dance with me?"

I had said it and it didn't hurt as bad as I thought it would. My heart was racing but my mind grew calmer as I waited for her answer. It was harder saying those words than waiting for her reply. It is always harder to break off a piece of beef jerky and chew it than it is to swallow it once you have been jawing on it. We sat there on that breezy afternoon, in her front yard, and looked each other directly in the eyes as if everything around us had become a blur. We existed in a blue and green orb. We were the center of a maelstrom and it was calm within our domain. I could see her luscious lips parting as she spoke to me and her eyes never wavered from mine, locked like true lovers, as she replied, "Oh, you are so sweet. I don't dance. Jade asked me the other night if I was going to the dance and I told her about our trip. We will be out of town that weekend. We're going to San Antonio for a family trip, you know. I'm sorry."

I tried not to let on about how disappointed I felt on the inside so I just said, with a fake smile on my face, "Oh, okay, I don't dance much either. I probably won't even go. I bet you'll like San Antonio. Have you ever been there?"

As I smiled at her and talked, I felt like my heart was floating upside down in an old fishbowl. I really wanted to take Rae to the Indian Dance. I had daydreamed a hundred times about slow dancing with her on the hardwood gym floor. I had thought so much about it I could almost feel her in my arms even if I had never held her close. I tried to block out my disappointment and continued jibber-jabbering to her about San Antonio. Rae smiled back at me and I couldn't tell if she knew how much the asking of her to go to the dance meant to me or not. She just replied, sweetly, "Really, I am sorry, about the dance. No, I haven't ever been to San Antonio. I'm not looking forward to spending the trip with my parents, that will be a drag, you know. So what is so great about San Antonio?"

"Ha!" I shouted, "San Antonio is great! Of course you'll just have to go see the Alamo. It is in the center of town. They have a lot of old cannons there. The Alamo is so famous. Did you ever see the movie about the Alamo? Jim Bowie died at the Alamo, you know the man who invented the Bowie knife. Colonel Travis and Davey Crockett or was it Daniel Boone, anyway, one of those two wilderness hunting men died in the fight against Santa Anna and the Spanish army at the Alamo. That's what the whole thing was about. If I remember from junior high in old man Sumrall's Texas History class, the Alamo was actually an old mission, sort of like a church, and the Texas army holed up in there to fight this massive Mexican army led by General Santa Anna. I always thought it was funny a Mexican General had a girl's name like Anna."

Rae laughed at this part and so I got encouraged and just kept right on talking, "The Alamo isn't a church anymore, now it's more like a museum, but it is pretty cool. Oh, and San Antonio is the "king" of Mexican food restaurants. You do like Mexican food, right?"

Rae frowned and said, "No, it tastes like hot peppers."

She paused a minute while I stared at her, since I couldn't quite conceive anyone not liking my favorite food, and then she laughed, "Just kidding, I love Mexican food. I'm a regular tamale eater anonymous!"

I was surprised by her quick wit and also I was caught off guard by her humor. I laughed at myself and started up my San Antonio discussion again. "Well, you'll love eating in San Antonio! You have to try and go down on the River Walk. They have great restaurants and shops and all sorts of stuff on the River Walk. It kind of looks like those pictures of Italy, where they have rivers going through the city instead of roads and people ride in boats through the buildings. I forget if that is Venice, Italy or Florence. I know it's not Rome, though. So go down to the River Walk it is very cool and it's where all the people go at night. Oh, Rae, try and go to the zoo. They have got a fantastic zoo there, it was built in an old rock quarry and right next to the zoo is the Sunken Gardens. Those gardens are great too with waterfalls and fountains and lots of huge Koi goldfish! Dang! I wish I was going to San Antonio!"

Rae stared at me like I was crazy. She started to smile and said, "I never knew you had so much knowledge locked up your country boy head. I guess you like San Antonio from the way you get so excited. You are way more excited than I am about going there."

I listened to her speaking but my mind was absorbing her pretty face. Her teeth were so white and perfect and her skin a beautiful blend of tan and brown, contrasting with her gorgeous blonde hair. I tried to concentrate on her words but my mind called up images of holding her in a dark gym, dancing slow to love ballads on a floor strewn with confetti and sawdust. Finally I blinked at the sun and said, "Rae, you'll have fun. Did I ever tell you about the first time we ever made a trip to San Antonio?"

"No, I don't think I ever heard about it, but I guess you are going to tell me."

She laughed again at this. Her laughter was so musical, so honest. It was a good thing, because Rae was not the kind of girl that laughed very much. She always seemed to be so introspective and serious. It was a pleasure to be spending so much time with her. To see her smiling and laughing like this made me seem like I was floating above us and watching from the sky. It made me feel like maybe this was only another daydream. I laughed along with Rae. I stopped laughing long enough to reply, "Yes, I'm going to tell you about it. It was a long time ago. I still remember how disappointed that trip made me. It all happened when I was just a little kid. Do you remember hearing about Hurricane Carla? Well, it was the biggest hurricane to hit Texas since the great 1900 Storm hit Galveston! We all had to evacuate the coast so we loaded up and drove to San Antonio. I remember we stayed with some friends of my parents but I couldn't tell you who they were. I was too little to remember much of the trip but I remember one thing. Driving, on the way, my mom and dad said when we got to San Antonio we could go to the zoo. Of course since I loved animals and especially loved going to the zoo I got way too excited and got my hopes way too high. So you can see what was coming. We arrived in San Antonio and I said, "Yeah! Let's go to the zoo!"

I hadn't figured on one thing. Hurricane Carla had followed with torrential rains! So we had to stay inside the whole trip! I never saw the zoo or anything else in San Antonio! I will always remember Hurricane Carla and our San Antonio trip. I still get disappointed when I think about it!"

We were both quiet then. A cool breeze slipped between us like an invisible barrier and Rae looked up at the sky. I followed her gaze and saw purple martins slashing through the air, eating insects on the wing. From this distance they seemed like flat black bats or far away fighter jets. Rae watched the martins tuck their dark wings in quick bursts of speed and I watched her blue-green eyes. They seemed to me deeper than a lush tropical rainforest. I was swallowed up in those eyes and didn't snap out of it until she looked away from the sky and at me. She said, quietly, "Well, I don't think there will ever be another Hurricane Carla. Hurricane Rae, maybe."

She laughed quietly too and said, "Well, thanks for asking me to the dance. I have to go in now."

She reached over and kissed me on the cheek. Rae got up and walked quickly towards her house. She looked back once and waved a small hand towards me in a slow goodbye. I was still sitting where she had left me and I waved back as she went inside her house and the door creaked closed. My skin burned hot like fire where her lips had kissed me. I stood up a little dizzy and I felt as if maybe I could fly like the purple martins. Rae dominated my every thought it seemed. I would go to the dance and watch everyone have fun but my heart would be in San Antonio with Rae.

"TALKING WAS HIS MOST POWERFUL WEAPON."

The Kimmings family was in San Antonio the night of the Indian Dance and I went alone, knowing I would see some of my friends there. I wasn't a very fashionable dresser so I changed shirts about five times. I ended up wearing my favorite faded blue jeans and a dark black collared shirt. I thought I was very cool in tennis shoes and jeans. The gym was decorated with crepe paper streamers and lots of green and gold balloons. The cheerleaders had made plenty of signs and the student council had provided the refreshment stand with the funds going to the Senior class. I walked in, searching for my friends from school, and purchased a ticket from a mousy girl named Beth at the entrance table. She smiled at me and I smiled back, even though I could almost see right through her because all I could ever see these days was Rae's face in front of my eyes.

I entered the darkened gym. I heard the low rumble of the bass speakers as rock music blared and reverberated in the place. Led Zeppelin's "Black Dog" cranked out and I could feel the vibrations in the floor. I saw a crowd of football players and made my way over to them expecting to see either Terry or Skip Howing. I didn't really hang around Skip but he always hung around Terry so we ended up in the same crowd frequently. Skip was extremely thin and agile. He was like a spider monkey and he chattered like one too. Skip was a talker.

Talking was his most powerful weapon. Skip could talk down the biggest guy from punching him in the face. If you were in a crowd that included Skip, you might as well zip your lips and become a spectator and a listener because that boy would dominate the world around you with his mouth.

I remember going in an old blue car that Skip drove around to Texas City. He called his car, which was a 1970 blue Nova, the "blue duck." We had played football all day long out in Terry's dad's sheep pasture and that night we were planning to cruise the Texas City strip. Actually the strip was really called Palmer Highway or Highway 1764, but teenagers called it the strip. The cars would be going up and down Palmer Highway, guys hanging out of cars trying to get girl's phone numbers or talking them into going out to the Old Blue Hole. It was a great spot for teenagers to go parking. The Old Blue Hole was located way out on the eastern part of town near the Texas City Dike. You could see Galveston Island across the water from the dike. I called, "shotgun" and sat up front on the passenger's side window while Skip drove the "blue duck." Terry was in back with another friend who sometimes ran around with us named, Howie Wolfe. Howie was a football player like the rest of us but Howie was our tough guy. We liked to bring Howie along because he was big and he could fight. In school he beat up so many guys that they started calling him "werewolf."

The only thing that bothered me about Howie Wolfe was that he always liked to pop you with what he called "friendly punches." He would see you in the hall at school and zap a hard fist into your arm. I used to get bruised up pretty good sometimes. I have always wondered if he still went around in his adult life popping the crap out of people he works with? I think if I was his boss, the first time Howie Wolfe hits me in the arm with a "friendly punch," is when he gets fired.

Texas City is only about fifteen minutes away and the guys in the Santa Fe School had an unwritten rule. The unwritten rule goes something like this; if you dated a girl from a town other than your own, the guys think you are major cool but the girls from your own town really get upset with you. You can actually get black-balled from dating girls in your own school if you have a reputation for dating out of town girls.

I wasn't experienced with girls much yet anyway but my friends were always out chasing what they called "poontang." I seemed to always be too involved with camping out in the woods or catching wildlife or drawing animals. I did like to tag along for the Saturday night joy rides down the strip, even if I was scared half-to death most of the time. I worried that I would get beat up by some monster Texas City football player or I worried that we would get thrown in jail for driving crazy or something. With Howie along and Skip driving anything could happen.

We left the cow-town behind and headed for the Texas City strip. Howie kept punching Terry in the arm in the back seat and I could hear Skip's terrible singing to the Ohio Players on the radio. I ignored the back seat commotion and stuck my head out the window, letting the cool breeze blast my face. It felt good. I thought to myself, "now I know why dogs always put their heads out of the cars window."

Skip said that a girl was killed while the Ohio Players were recording "Love Rollercoaster" and that you could hear her scream in the background of the song. I listened closely when he turned it up but I never did hear anybody dying in the song. I let the wind beat against my face and Howie spoke up from the back seat and I glanced back there to see Terry rubbing his arm. I was so glad I didn't sit back there. Howie said, "Hey, dudes, let's cruise the strip a few times, stop at the library parking lot and at the "turn around" in the Weingarten's parking lot and hang out. Last week Dale Teknic told me about the Texas City cheerleaders cruising the Weingarten's parking lot."

Weingarten's was a grocery store almost at the end of the strip where everyone turned around. Sometimes people parked there to hang out and yell at each other. A lot of fights took place there too. The police were always cruising down there too, chasing all the teenagers away, and telling them to keep moving.

We made it to Texas City and roared onto the strip in the "blue duck." This was a typical Saturday night and the strip was full of cars loaded down with teenagers. We hollered at the cars that drove next to us with girls in them and they of course hollered back. Howie pulled down his jeans once and mooned a car full of fat girls. We were all laughing so hard Skip almost ran the "blue duck" into the back of a Ford pickup truck at the Jack in the Box intersection. The girls liked getting mooned because they started following us everywhere we drove. We pulled into the library parking lot and they pulled in beside us. Skip was going to peel out when they stopped but Howie told him not to because he thought the girl in their back seat was cute. They pulled up and the driver, a fat cheeked girl with pretty eyes, said, "hey ya'll, what's ya'lls names?"

I didn't say anything but Skip shouted out his name, "Skip baby, Skip you!"

He peeled out after that and Howie, standing next to the car, was still hanging onto the open door as it was jerked out of his hand. Skip drove crazily through the parking lot and back out onto the strip. I yelled at him and so did Terry, "Hey, stupid! You just left Howie back there!"

Skip laughed, "So what. Maybe he'll get lucky. He can

find his own way home. I didn't want to stop and talk to those losers anyway."

We never saw Howie again that night but the next week at school he said he was glad we left him there with those girls. He said they felt as if it was their fault that he got left behind so they let him ride around with them up and down the strip. He told us he rode in the backseat with the cute girl and necked most of the time. He tried to get them to go out to the Old Blue Hole but the driver girl refused, but at least he got a ride home. He started going steady with that cute Texas City girl but I heard they broke up when she found out he was going steady with a girl in Santa Fe and another girl in Galveston.

At the Indian Dance I was standing around talking to Terry, Skip, and two other guys, Tony Tiggerino, and Dennis Fevers. Tony was the king premier of the FFA, the Future Farmers Association and before high school he had been king of the junior 4H club. I think he won Grand Champion Steer at least ten times at the Galveston County Fair and Rodeo. Tony was slow in the girlfriend department because he always had to tend to his father's ranch and he was always raising cattle. The coaches always tried to get him to play football because he was so large but his father said he couldn't because he needed his help on the ranch. I once saw Tony bench press two freshmen kids lying on top of him. He later tried to bench press three freshmen but he couldn't balance them correctly. Tony was a good old boy. He was just big and playful and not the smartest thing on two legs. We all liked Tony but nobody liked his dad. There were a lot of rumors that his dad beat him and his mom with regularity.

The other guy hanging out with our crowd at the Indian Dance was Dennis Fevers. Dennis was tall and lanky and liked to work on cars. He could fix any car. He had long hair like the lead singer of the "Doobie Brothers." He used to wear a wig to school and tuck his long stringy hair up in it because our school had a strict dress code. The dress code rule about hair was that a boy's hair could not touch your shirt collar or your ears. The barbershops in Santa Fe got rich back then in the sixties and the seventies. My father used to take my brother and I to a barbershop over in the neighboring town of Pearland to a scary barbershop. It was scary because they cut your hair with these electric clippers that had vacuum cleaner hoses on them. As they cut the hair, the vacuum sucked it up into bags on the wall. I was told that they sold the hair to wig shops. I kept thinking that some old lady somewhere in New York City was walking around town wearing a wig made out of my cut off hair. That always scared me. I don't really know why.

I saw Jade Morgan and Leslie Gertone, Rae's druggie friends. I saw my favorite teacher, Coach Easterly, and he came over to us. He taught History and I loved his class. He shook all our hands, and he said, "Hey boys, it is a nice dance this year."

I agreed, as did Terry, but Skip, who didn't like Coach Easterly because he had gotten swatted for losing the lock for his gym locker only grunted and looked away. Howie said, in his usual smart mouth way, "Sure coach whatever you say."

Coach said, as he turned and went to seek out Miss Lilac, the new English teacher for a dance, "okay boys, stay out of trouble and trouble will stay away from you."

I always remember his words and I didn't know it then but I know it now, I took those words to heart and kept them always within an oyster shell's throw away. I repeated those words to myself. "Stay out of trouble and trouble will stay away from you."

Terry went off to dance with a cute Latino girl named, Rosa, and Skip teamed up with Howie, Tony and Dennis to pick on the Martian boys. I stayed back a few steps from them while they harassed the Martian boys. I was always nervous about bothering the Martian boys, partially because maybe I thought they really did come from Mars but mostly because I didn't want to get in trouble. The Martian boys names were Johnathan Fleming and Theodore Harris. They were both straight A students and they both were always carrying briefcases with them all over the school. Johnathan and Theodore both wore black horn-rimmed glasses and carried pocket calculators in their front pockets. They both also wore bow ties to school frequently, and they wore dress slacks always. I don't think they even owned a pair of blue jeans. Both of the Martian boys plastered their short hair down with some kind of grease in an "old" man style. The reason they were called the Martian boys is because they talked in strange noises to each other. They also told anyone who would listen that they were from Mars. If any of the guys in school started harassing them they would start talking in their bleeps and beeps and began blinking their eyes and moving their fingers over their heads in weird gestures.

I had the taller one, Johnathan, in my History class and he would open his briefcase and shuffle the tons of papers he had in there all through class. He would always cover his papers with his arm and by leaning over into the open briefcase. I guess he thought everyone would try to look at what he had in there. Once I saw a bunch of the football players chasing the Martian boys across the football field during lunchtime. Johnathan and Theodore were running awkwardly, looking like two ducks with wooden legs, with about six or seven football players chasing them and hollering at them to stop. The Martian boys were squawking and screeching their Martian language as they ran. They were carrying those heavy briefcases in one arm like they were loaded down with gold bars. The other arm was in the air making Martian gestures like they were calling their flying saucer to come pick them up.

I heard later that the reason they were being chased is because Joey Lambertson, the all-district lineman, had caught them peeking in the boy's showers of the field house. He grabbed his shorts and shouted at some of the other football guys and they went after the Martian boys. Both of the Martian boys talked with lisps and were very polite to their teachers. I never remember hearing them talk with the bleeps and beeps to any of the teachers, I guess they didn't want any of the adults to know they were from Mars.

As I watched Dennis and the others start mouthing off to the Martian boys a girl I didn't know snuck up behind me. I felt a tap on my shoulder and so I turned around, expecting one of my friends but instead there was this very short, petite girl behind me. She had the biggest eyes I have ever seen. She almost looked like one of Santa's elf-girl helpers. She was probably only about four feet nine with the reddest hair, the color red like when you look deep into a campfire that is almost out but still smoldering, and you see those red flickering embers under the burnt logs. I said, "Hi."

She smiled, revealing pretty white teeth and dimples on her olive skin. She said, "Hello, want to dance this song with me?"

I was caught off-guard and stuttered, "Uh, sure, what is it, Moody Blues?"

The small girl took my hand and led me out on the dance floor. She told me her name was Toni. I wasn't a very good dancer but she guided me around and put her head on my shoulder. Her hair smelled nice and it felt good to move around with this little elf girl. I started to get into this slow dancing song and just when I was getting comfortable the song ended. We stepped apart from each other and she said, "Thank you, will you come get me and dance with me again later?"

I smiled at her and replied, "Sure Toni. It was fun."

I walked back to where the other guys were surrounding the Martian boys. The Martian boys did not have their briefcases with them. I wondered why they would even come to a dance. As I approached I heard Dennis say, "Okay, you little nerd-freaks, stop talking that alien mess and answer me now!"

Johnathan and Theodore just blabbered incoherent ramblings of their Martian language until Dennis pushed Theodore. Theodore fell backwards onto the punch table, knocking the big punch bowl into one of the chairs behind the table. A big splash of punch burst out of the bowl as it was knocked down and landed on Missy Harkens. She was instantly drenched and started crying like a baby. Her dress was white and now she was pink and wet and soaked thoroughly. We could all see through her dress and her sheer bra. That was the first time I had ever seen a girl's breasts. She didn't seem to notice that she was entered in her first wet T-shirt contest unknowingly and continued to stand there and cry and drip punch from her wet hair and dress. Theodore fell over the table and landed on his stomach on the other side. His glasses fell off and I saw someone dancing, accidentally step on them. The right lens shattered and the dancer's boot crunched the glass as he glided by. Watching his Martian friend get pushed over, Johnathan seemed to go into an agitated fit. Dennis and the others started backing up from the Martian boy as he chattered incoherently in that Martian gibberish. I saw Coach Easterly approaching and Miss Lilac was close behind him. I saw Dennis start to push Johnathan but Howie grabbed him and said, "We need to get the heck out of here, now!"

People had started to crowd around the scene and I was backing up, not wanting to have anything to do with it. Johnathan ran forward at Dennis with the punch ladle in his hand, swinging it like a club. I could hear Missy crying and Johnathan squawking and the music playing was Jethro Tull. I saw Johnathan swing the punch ladle and it connected with Dennis's nose with a loud crack. Dennis howled, trying to get loose from Howie's grasp. Johnathan said, "Go away, puny earthling, beep, beep, beep."

Theodore crawled over the table and I could see punch stains on his white shirt. Theodore's face was drawn in a grimace, his rosy cheeks flustered to a violent red smear. Theodore walked past Johnathan to attack Dennis but Coach Easterly stepped in between them.

I had never before seen the Martian boys ever fight back. I was amazed. The Martian boys always just took whatever punishment or harassment was given to them. I guess they got pushed too far this time. Suddenly all the lights in the gym went out. I heard a rumbling sound outside. I felt a cold chill crawl all over my skin. I knew what this was now. I just knew what was happening. The Martian boys flying saucer was rumbling outside the gym waiting to pick them up and to fire death rays at us humans for tormenting their comrades. Any second I expected to see the gym roof blasted off and a floating giant flying saucer hovering above us. The lights came back on in a series of flickers and I heard the thunder outside again. It was just a storm moving in. The Martian boys had moved away from us and started talking to one another in that strange babbling language. Coach Easterly was really in Dennis's face, chewing him out. I decide to make my get away from this crowd before I got in trouble by association.

I made my way across the crowded gym to the other side. I

was looking for my new friend, Toni. I liked dancing with her, even though I didn't really know how to dance properly. She made me feel like I knew what I was doing. I saw her by the FFA girls. She didn't look like a cowgirl but she was standing in their crowd. Toni was wearing hip-hugger, bell-bottom jeans and the FFA girls all wore Wrangler's and boots. Toni saw me coming and said, happily, "Hey, I know you. You're that good dancer from the other side of the gym."

I started laughing, because she had a big kidding smile on her cute face and also because it made me less nervous. I chuckled and replied, "That's me, the dancing fool. So, what do you say? Do you want to try it again, dancing slow to the next good song?"

As I talked to her I saw beyond her by the soft drink machines, Jade Morgan and Leslie Gertone. They glanced at me and then resumed their bad posture talking to some of their druggie friends. Toni grabbed my hand and pulled me on the dance floor. I don't know why but as I followed this cute girl I saw Rae's face in my mind. I was dancing to a romantic Chicago song with Toni and my thoughts were drifting away to San Antonio and Rae. I imagined her sitting up in their hotel room, reading Anne Sexton poetry by lamplight. I wonder if she thought of me at all. I danced quite a few songs with Toni that night and had mastered a few steps of my own as she taught me to two-step to the right songs. I remember that night because of the Martian boys fighting back, Missy's wet-T shirt contest, learning to dance better with Toni, and the terrible tragedy later that evening while I was home sleeping, dreaming of Rae in San Antonio.

"...A TERRIBLE CAR ACCIDENT ON HIGHWAY 6."

The next morning my mom told me that there had been a terrible car accident on Highway 6. Jade Morgan and Leslie Gertone were dead. Rory Marks and Fred McGlocum were in the hospital. Fred was in critical condition still in the I.C.U. Rory would be out in a day. He wasn't even hurt, just bruised. My mom told her that Janet McGlocum was also admitted because she was in shock. The newspaper didn't spread word around here as fast as the phone. Small Texas towns have a so many gossips, and it is why many do not even have a newspaper. Santa Fe was one of these. The only newspaper was the Galveston Daily News or the Texas City Sun. Santa Fe would later get a small newspaper but it would only last a decade or so before going out of business. It was called the Bulletin. My mom told me the news at the breakfast table. I couldn't believe it. Rae would be hurt. Leslie and Jade were her friends. My mom said, "Rory was driving that race car Camaro of his. They were all drinking alcohol. You better stay away from alcohol! Who knows what else those wild boys were doing. Fred got in trouble at school for marijuana before. Leslie and Jade left the dance last night with Rory and Fred. Someone said they were going to Galveston to ride on the seawall. They were going too fast through Hitchcock on Highway 6 on the way home. Hitchcock is such a dark town. They don't have hardly any street lights out near that old Flamingo Isles place.

They say someone had left a broken down trailer with an old boat on it on the side of the highway and Rory swerved onto the shoulder. He must have not seen the trailer with the boat. The cops said he was going over eighty miles an hour."

I was eating my cereal as my mom fretted and paced about the kitchen talking to me about the dangers of alcohol and wild driving. I couldn't quite grasp death yet. Leslie and Jade were gone. I went to church and had learned about Jesus and Heaven and wondered if those two girls were floating in the white clouds with angels. I didn't really know if Heaven had a different set of rules than Earth, like if alcohol was a sin or not? I tried not to imagine Leslie and Jade, burning up with flames in Hell with their arms around the waist of this red man with horns and a tail. I kept thinking about those two wild girls but mostly I thought about how Rae would feel when she found out about the tragedy. I didn't want to be the one to tell her. I ate my cereal and went outside to be by myself.

I climbed the hill by the lake and sat down on the hill's crest, above the chocolate water. Every once in a while the water would splash with some fish flapping his tail about. I sat up there in the hazy sunlight, partially shaded by a small twisted tallow tree. One of Rae's friends, a honeybee, buzzed around my face and then found some red and yellow flowers to land on. If Rae were here she would probably be talking to the bee. I listened to the many birds around me in the brush and the few trees. I could hear bobwhite quail out in the prairie and doves cooing in the trees. A loud mockingbird sang shrill songs copied from many other birds. A snapping turtle stuck his snout and eyes above the water and I thought about Mr. Kimmings getting excited about catching snapping turtles. I remembered those dead snapping turtles in his backyard and was glad he wasn't here to kill this smaller one. I thought about how Leslie and Jade had died. I heard my mom talking on the phone to her friend, Mrs. Lunny, and I heard that Jade's head got cut off in the accident. She also said that Leslie got thrown out of the car because she didn't have a seatbelt on. My imagination was going wild out here in the woods thinking about two dead girls and dead snapping turtles. The images of those dead snapping turtles, with their guts spilled out merged with the images of Leslie and Jade dead on Highway 6. I started crying. I wasn't really crying for the two girls and I know I wasn't crying for the dead snapping turtles but maybe I was crying about death itself.

I spent most of that day out by the lake until I finally got hungry and returned to my house. My mom had put some leftovers in the refrigerator so I took out the cold fried chicken at plopped down in front of the television. She left a note saying that they had gone to the store in Texas City. I ate cold fried chicken on that Sunday afternoon, trying not to think so much anymore about the wild girls dead on highway 6. I watched Bewitched, the television show about a good witch that married a human and they had a child named Tabitha who was a baby witch. Our black and white television was in the living room and I liked lying on the big oval rug while I ate. I usually could only do this if mom and dad were gone. They would holler and tell me, "Son, you don't eat on the floor, now get up and sit at the table like a respectable person!"

I always think about what they would say to me but even now at age forty-five I still recline on the floor in front of the television and eat cold chicken.

"I WAS STANDING OUT IN MY YARD CATCHING TOADS..."

Rae returned from San Antonio later in the week and she didn't come outside for weeks after that. I eventually didn't think as much about Leslie and Jade anymore but I did think about Rae. I wondered if she was going to be okay. She wasn't an inside kind of person. The tragedy of losing her two friends must be really hitting her hard. I was standing out in my yard catching toads when Terry walked up. I would look under the big rocks near the garden and find dark brown toads hiding and grab them. Toads are the slowest hopping creatures and even a child could catch them. If you don't hold a toad correctly you will be in trouble. The first thing a toad will do when captured is try to pee on you. My Paw Paw tried to make me believe that a toad's pee will give you warts wherever it touches your skin. He even showed me a wart on his arm where he said a big toad once peed. I can tell you right now I am either immune to toad's pee or the entire story of getting warts from toads is a farce because I have been peed on so many times catching toads. After learning of the toad's natural response to capture, I perfected a way of grabbing them that allows you to stay dry. The first thing a toad does when you discover where it is hiding is to hunch down and flatten its body. The toad thinks that by flattening down that you cannot see it blending in with the dirt. Of course the toad is wrong. Maybe this method might fool some animals that do not have very good eyesight but it doesn't fool people. While the toad flattens out, before he gives up on hiding and decides to start hopping slowly away, you quickly pin him down with your hand and then grab along his spine with two fingers. Picking up a toad by his back with two fingers lets the toad pee away as much as he wants to and it doesn't get on your skin but falls harmlessly to the ground.

The reason I mostly caught toads is because they were so plentiful and they were great food for my hognose snake. Hoggy was my snake's name and I had kept him out back in a terrarium for a few years. He loved fresh hopping toad for dinner. Toads are now on the endangered list in southern Texas and you don't see as many of them anymore. Every ditch and pond in Santa Fe used to have millions of toad tadpoles swimming like black minnows. We used to catch them by the bucketfuls and bring them home. We would raise baby toads in big bathtubs my dad had put in the ground in the rock garden. I can't remember a single time when we didn't have hundreds of toads hopping all over the grass and the pastures at night. Toads hide in the daylight and come out at night to eat bugs. One of the best experiences I ever had with toads happened back then when toads ruled the town.

It was in the summer and Terry and I were at a girl's softball game at Runge Park. It was a night game and we always went to check out all the cute teenage girls playing softball. When the game began to get boring we went walking around the park. We noticed that there were many toads hopping all over the place. I told Terry, "Let's catch as many as we can. I saw some paper bags over behind the dumpster. We can fill the bags up with toads!"

I ran and grabbed a couple of paper bags and we started grabbing as many toads as we could. We didn't even care if the toads peed on us, we just grabbed them as fast as we could. I had a plan form in my head as soon as I saw the bags getting filled up. We just kept on catching the hopping toads, chasing herds of them all around Runge Park. The toads were piled up on top of one another and the bags started to get heavy. Soon there were too many toads in the bags and they started hopping back out as soon as we put them in. I sat down my paper bag and shouted to Terry, "Okay! I think we have enough of them now!"

He said, "Maybe we should get more bags, I think we should catch all the toads in Runge Park and bring them to the zoo. They would probably pay us about a dollar a toad. I know we got at least five hundred dollars worth of toads already and there are hundreds hopping away all around us right now."

I just sat there holding my toad bag closed, feeling the toads hopping against the paper and stared at him. I gave him a stupid look and replied, "Yeah, we should sell toads to the zoo. I'm sure the Houston Zoo is holding a big fat wad of money right now to pay all the people to bring them toads. That's why people go to the zoo I'm sure, to see the dreaded captured Galveston County Toad. Terry, Terry, please get a grip. The zoo doesn't want toads unless they are exotic toads from Madagascar and the weigh about ten pounds each. I have a better idea and we don't need to catch anymore."

He laughed, "Yeah, the zoo don't need toads but they do pay for animals they need. So what are we gonna' do with all these toads?"

I laughed loudly and put my hands over my face. I pointed to the softball game and smiled big, saying, "Girls just love toads, don't they? Ha! Guess what would happen if thousands of millions of toads started hopping across the softball field. Do you know? Can you imagine? Girls would be pulling out their hair and screaming and running everywhere! It would be great! It would be the best event of our time! We are on the verge of greatness! Can you feel it? Are you with me? We are gonna' let all these toads go on the softball field. We will get behind home plate and dump out the bags!"

Terry scratched his head and thought about it for a minute. He started smiling too, "We will have to be quick."

We each grabbed our toad bags and carried them behind home plate just as Beckie Hibbins was batting. Everyone was watching the game. Nobody was paying attention to us as we sat by the fence right behind the umpire and positioned our toad bags. I told Terry, "On the count of three we open the bag and dump it slowly over, facing the field. The holes in the fence are perfect size for the toads to hop through."

I whispered, "One, two, three..."

We both started dumping toads all through the fence. It only took a few seconds for us to empty the bags and scramble up. We ran behind the bleachers to watch the hundreds of hopping toads make their way across the grass behind home plate. The umpire groaned, "Strike two!" Becky Hibbins swung her bat at the ball and missed. A few kids in the bleachers started to notice the hordes of toads edging towards home plate and spreading out beyond to the playing field. Becky was waiting on the next pitch when she looked down and saw a large toad hop right between her feet and land on home plate. Another fat toad landed on her shoe and that is when she screamed! That moment is also when we started laughing. The catcher, Pam Dodlin, threw her mask down trying to hit the toads with it. The umpire raised his hands and said, "Time out!"

The other girls started to notice why Becky was screaming and they ran off the field, heading towards the safety of the dugouts. The toad army was now covering the entire infield and the girls in each dugout were screaming their heads off. The coaches were trying not to laugh but I saw the umpire snickering. The coaches and the two umpires were conferring on the pitcher's mound as toads hopped all around their feet. At about this time I noticed people were pointing and staring at us. I guess they had figured out that we were responsible for the unleashing of the toad horde. I looked at Terry and he looked back at me, "Uh, I think we should get out of here! C'mon! Run!"

We ran off into the darkness turning off the asphalt roads into the pastures, away from the bright lights of Runge Park. No one would follow us into the dark desolation of the vast cow pastures of Santa Fe at night. We walked across the pastures, ducking under barbwire fences from time to time, all the way home. I still remember that great moment and think about it when I see toads hopping about, which is very rare today. We never even got in trouble for releasing toads at the softball field. I even read somewhere that toads are endangered in south Texas now, but then again Galveston and Harris County both have killed off so many native species I would be surprised if there are any native wild places left for any species of animal in the next ten years. If there is a space where trees grow wild and the land is isolated, there are native Texas animals squeezing in to try to find a tiny haven to survive. Those little spaces of trees, honey suckle vines, sticker bushes, blackberry vines and brambles are few now and as soon as each new developer decides they need another million dollars to build a new subdivision, they bulldoze it all, trees too. I am ashamed of this part of the world, but that is another story, growing up in southern Texas was a better life back then. Rae was here and the wind still had the smell of honey suckle.

"I WAS AFRAID TO MOVE."

I finally saw Rae outside after a few weeks had passed since the funerals of Leslie and Jade. It was Saturday afternoon and it was pouring rain. It had been raining for two days and I didn't see any chance of it ever stopping. I liked rain. I liked the ditches filling up with water. I liked that way the rice canals flowed like gigantic rivers. I would go down to the rice canal and watch the big snakes swimming in the swirling water. I liked the way snakes swim and I liked to see all the different kinds of snakes that would show up driven from the holes in the ground by the flood waters. The rain slowed, drizzling, but it was airy and breezy outside. The ditches were already full of muddy water. The back pasture was starting to look like a vast lake dotted with islands. I wasn't in the mood for catching crawdads but there were plenty of them crawling under the shallow water in the flooded pasture. Today I wanted to go check out how much water was in our back drainage ditch. I liked when it got so full a miniature waterfall would form where it flowed into the larger ditch on the west side of the pasture. The sound of the rushing water was a pleasant sound and I still like it today.

I was barefoot and the cool water felt good as I walked in the flooded pasture. The water covered my ankles and I splashed and kicked water as I headed for the barn. The cattle were huddled underneath the big tree that was shaped liked an umbrella. They looked at me and started to follow me. I knew what the cattle were wanting. They followed me thinking it was feeding time. Anytime somebody goes to the barn they always think its time to eat. I walked past the barn as the cattle slowly walked into it. They had been fooled but at least they had better shelter from the rain under the tin roof, besides they always had hay to munch on inside the barn. I saw a scissor-tailed flycatcher perched on the barbwire fence as I came around the corner of the barn. My dad built our barn by hand, hammer and saw. He had built many barns, each one looking mostly the same as the last. He would build them out of rusty tin and lumber. He never painted any of the barns like the red ones you see in northern states. Our barns were purely Texas style cattle barns, rust and flat gray, a little silver when the sun hits the metal just right. I saw gray, white and a dash of a black tail that flashed down the ravine as the scissor-tailed flycatcher flew away. The native Texas scissor-tailed flycatcher is a beautiful and unusual bird. They have very long split tails twice as long as their gray body, which is about the size of the Texas state bird, the mockingbird. They often perch on fence wire waiting for flying insects. Usually where there was one flycatcher there was another one not far away. It seems like I would always see them in pairs. I thought it unusual that there was only one flying away in the drizzle.

I stood on the bank of the rushing water and watched as foam and bubbles floated by. I knew with this much water flowing that a hundred yards to the west would be the little waterfall. I started following the ravine along the banks of the rushing water and that's why I saw her. Rae was sitting in the rain, soaking wet, in a stand of tall, matted wheat grass. She didn't see me. I stopped and froze, excited and alarmed. Rae was an enigma. She was drenched and sitting alone in the tall grass. She sat Indian style with her legs in a weird yoga position. Her blonde hair was dark, dripping wet. Her white shirt was transparent and clung to her like a second skin. Rae had blue jean shorts on and little leather sandals. She seemed to be staring at the distant woods. My heart was pounding. Finding her in such a bizarre situation made me feel as if I had stumbled upon some strange magic ritual. I felt the cold wet raindrops hitting my skin but inside I was burning up, like a potholder left too close to the stove. I could not take my eyes from the wet girl sitting in the grass. This discovery was like finding an albino unicorn in a secret forest. I felt like an intruder and I knew I should get away from here but my eyes were magnetized to the magic of Rae.

I couldn't bring myself to leave so I sat down in the mud and the rocks alongside the rushing water. I became very still and settled in to watch Rae. I was so still and quiet that the scissor-tailed flycatcher eventually came back and landed once again on the barbwire fence. I had been sitting in the drizzling rain for about ten minutes when I heard a sob escape from Rae. Her shoulders were shaking. It hurt me on the inside to see her so upset. Without thinking I stood up and started across the water, splashing in the thigh deep ditch. Rae heard me coming and turned to look. I stopped in the middle of the rushing water when her eyes met mine. I couldn't move and I was afraid, nervous, wondering what she was thinking. I didn't say anything as I looked into her mysterious beautiful eyes. The eyes of a unicorn, speckled with no distinct dominant color. Her eyes were like raindrops filled with flecks from rainbows. Rae's eyes stared into my soul and I felt like a helpless deer watching a hunter settle the cross of the scope on his rifle on my heart. I waited for her to say something to end this stalemate of vision. She remained quiet and then looked away from me. She stared once again at the nearby woods. The edge of the greenery was about fifty yards across the cow pasture. I followed her gaze to the large tree that dominated the woods. I had always liked this huge old tree and had clambered up into its thick limbs many times. There wasn't another tree as big as this one for miles. I looked through the falling rain and for the first time noticed that there was something on the lowest branch. I squinted my eyes to see better, and I discovered that a scraggly brown bobcat was standing in the crotch of the tree trying to stay out of most of the rain under the trees sheltering branches. The bobcat was looking in our direction. I figured he could probably see us but he didn't jump down and run.

Rae put her head down into her hands and started wiping her face. Her tears would mingle with the rain but she tried to wipe her face dry anyway. I alternately watched the big bobcat and Rae. I was afraid to move. This was one of those moments that you would never forget the rest of your life. This was a moment where time really just stopped. I was sure that if I had a watch on I could have looked at it and it would have frozen. The only thing moving was the water around my legs and the rain slightly falling. I don't even think I was breathing.

Suddenly, a massive lightning strike flashed extremely close, followed by a blast of monstrous, deafening thunder. I saw Rae flinch, startled by the thunder, and I jumped back. I looked at the tree near the woods and saw that the old bobcat was gone. Time, I knew, had begun again.

I started to say something to her but she turned away from me and I could see her shivering. I wanted to go to her and hold her but I was afraid. I do not know what I was afraid of, Rae's sadness or my own reaction to being close to her. I could feel the cold water swirling around my legs and it had started to rain harder. I looked one last time at Rae, wet and shivering sitting in the wet grass of the cow pasture. I walked slowly out of the water and headed in the opposite direction with my head down and my heart confused. The rain was pelting down in a thundering torrent now and I hunched over as I headed for the safety of the screened porch. My mother was folding clothes on the porch and said, when she saw me outside in the pouring rain, "Get in here out of the storm! Are you crazy? You are soaking wet! Here, take this towel and dry off and I'll get you some clean clothes."

Mom went into the house and I stripped out of my wet clothes and wrapped the thick towel around me, waiting for her to bring me some dry clothes. She returned carrying the clothes and I took them and went into our garage to change as she said, "Try to stay dry this time and stay inside, please. In about an hour that television show about Amazon wildlife will be on channel 8."

I dressed and came back out onto the screened porch and sat in a wicker chair, watching my mother fold clothes. Our parakeets, Reno and Vegas, chirped and whistled in their tall wire cage, trying to get our attention. I liked to listen to Reno and Vegas and I always imagined that when I mimicked their sounds that they could understand me. My mom would just shake her head as I talked to the two parakeets. Reno was bright yellow and Vegas was blue and white. We used to have a different blue parakeet, named Tahoe, but our big tabby cat, Lossi, got his paw in the cage and killed it. Lossi eventually prowled too far away from home one day and never came back, so the parakeets were safe now. I used to let them out inside the house and they would sit on my shoulder. My mother didn't like it because they would fly like crazy and land on things that were breakable. The parakeets also didn't mind using the bathroom in the house either. I haven't let them out in a long time now since Vegas bit my earlobe and made it bleed.

My mother and I watched the rain pour down through the screen of our porch and we talked of school and sports. I learned that my dad was a good football player in high school. He played football when they only wore leather helmets without the protective bars of a face-mask. The thought of playing football in pads without bars protecting your face is kind of scary, but I would have played it anyway. Later I went inside carrying my folded clothes and put them away just in time to sit down and watch the National Geographic special about the Amazon River wildlife. I enjoyed learning about Piranha, capybara, tapirs and jaguars.

Later that night I was awake in my bed thinking about Rae sitting out there in the pouring rain. I thought about her tears blending with the rain on her face and about how her eyes looked. I lay awake a long time, listening to the light rain outside my window until I finally fell asleep. That night I had a dream that I remembered as I awoke, a dream that I can still see as if it were a black and white movie on an old rabbit-eared television set.

I stood on a beach with great disturbing waves rolling in. The sky was dark and gray even though it was early in the day. The gray and charcoal clouds moved rapidly in the turbulent sky. It seemed like there wasn't any color in the world, only a gray wash on everything. I could see seagulls trying to fly in the strong winds and they seemed about as lost as a sailboat without sails trying to make way around Cape Horn. The beach around me was empty and void of life except for the chaotic seagulls. As isolated as I seemed I was disturbed and anxious as I watched each great wave crest and roll towards the beach. My feet were bare and the sand seemed to suck my skin down farther with each wave. I saw my grandmother and grandfather, Noni and Paw Paw, walking down the beach towards me. I cupped my hands to my mouth and shouted to them, "Noni! Paw Paw! Over here!"

They didn't hear me and walked out into the waves. I shouted, "Come back! Come back! I love you!"

They held hands in the ocean and kept walking until I couldn't see them anymore. Terror and sadness filled me. I was in a panic but my feet wouldn't move, stuck up to my ankles in the sand. The waves roared louder and the wind whipped my shirt and my hair. I strained my eyes to see far out into the ocean but I only saw more waves cresting and rolling in to the beach. I whispered, "Noni, Paw Paw, come back!"

I could still see their footprints in the sand where they had turned to walk out into the Gulf of Mexico. A sandpiper scurried along the shoreline and ran across their tracks. A salty tear ran down my face. The wind hurt my eyes. Everything was so gray. Inside I was sick and panicky. I saw a black cloud rumbling towards the beach and suddenly thunder crashed. A jagged bolt of lightning shimmered in the air. I put my hands up before my face and when I looked at the ocean again it was different. The waves roared like angry tigers with white claws scratching the sky. I looked at the water in front of me, and about twenty yards away at the edge of the ocean was a body lying sideways on the beach. It was a female and her face looked directly up into the gray sky. Her arms were crossed on her chest like an "x" and I thought maybe she was sleeping.

I walked closer to the still woman lying on her back. The waves rolled in and the water lapped at the woman's side. I saw that it was Rae. I stumbled back and almost fell down in the wet sand. The wind howled and the waves rumbled like an angry volcano. I put my hands up, covering my face. Rae was lying prone in the sand as the water washed up onto her, splashing and soaking her cotton dress and her long hair. The sand around her seemed to be causing a depression, sucking her body down into the very granules. A mournful wail filled the air and I thought it came from inside my head until I saw a black-headed laughing gull circling overhead. The ocean's waves threw mist at me and my clothes were beginning to get wet. I shivered and strode forward slowly, each step I could feel my heartbeat surging against my chest. I approached the still body of Rae, my eyes never leaving her face. Her eyes were closed and I knew she had to be dead.

I stood over her body, looking down at her beauty. She seemed so peaceful. My face was wet from the ocean and from my own tears. My clothes were drenched now and I was cold. I knelt down beside Rae and reached out to brush back the strands of wet hair that had covered her forehead. Rae opened her eyes.

I fell over backwards in the sand. She turned her head and smiled at me. I saw beyond her and discovered movement in the water. I was horrified as multi-legged blue and red crabs as big as cats scrambled out of the surf like scurrying armored spiders. Rae kept smiling at me even as a wave washed over her body and water splashed up into her face. The army of scary crabs marched out of the water and headed directly for Rae and I. I crawled backwards in horror. Hundreds of laughing gulls began to circle overhead like small albino vultures. The laughing of the gulls was loud even over the roar of the waves crashing. Rae stood up slowly. She looked to be levitated upwards until her bare feet were inches off the ground. The armored blue-shelled crabs, clicking their wicked heavy pinchers, circled her and bobbed like dancers on their jointed red legs. Rae spread her arms out from her body as the rain began to pour harder. I could barely see with the sheets of rain obscuring my eyes. Rae hung in the air like a living crucifix. She reached out a hand for me and the crabs parted their dancing circle. I stepped away from her, afraid. It was like the ocean became calm instantly. The rain stopped and Rae once again stood on the sand. The red and blue crabs retreated back into the water. Rae looked back at me and I could see that she was crying. Her eyes held mine momentarily and then she turned away. I said, "Rae, wait..."

She began walking out into the calm Gulf of Mexico. I started to go to her but my feet were stuck in the deepening sand of the beach. The gulls were gone and the sky turned blue as Rae walked deeper into the water. I saw her blonde hair go under the water and I tried to run out in the surf to save her. She was gone. The fury of the gulf came back as soon as my feet touched the water. A massive wave hit me in the face and bounced me back to shore. I fell onto the sand dunes and thrashed about.

That's when I woke up, tangled in my sheets with my pillows on the floor. It was still raining outside. I never forgot that dream. My Noni and Paw Paw are gone now and I still miss them. When I look out into the Gulf of Mexico I think about how I could see them in my dream holding hands on the beach. The dream kept me awake for quite awhile that night and the next day I was not as energetic as usual.

"WELL, WELL, MY DEAD SNAPPING TURTLE PARTNER."

The very next Saturday morning Mr. Kimmings was outside loading his truck with fishing supplies. I crossed the yard and said, "Hi, Mr. Kimmings! Are you going fishing today?"

He turned, a bit startled by my loud shout, and replied, with a light chuckle, "Well, well, my dead snapping turtle partner. Actually I'm going down to the canal to check my turtle lines and maybe cast a few hooks for whatever might be biting this pretty day."

I glanced at the sun, barely over the horizon, climbing higher by the second, and replied, "Kenny Bulbear told me last week he had a giant alligator gar on his line. He swore it was at least ten feet long. He told me he fought it for about half an hour and it finally broke his line. Kenny said that if the line wouldn't have broke the monster gar would have pulled him in. I have never seen a gar that big but I have heard they get even bigger than that."

Mr. Kimmings smiled, his wide nose got even wider and he laughed deeply, "Oh Kenny probably got tangled in a underwater tree by a wary wise old channel catfish. Heck, maybe even a big alligator snapping turtle got his hook. I have never caught a big alligator snapping turtle on my lines. There are plenty common snapping turtles in the canals but if I could ever catch one of those giant alligator snappers we could have a feast. One of those big alligator snappers could feed the poor and you and me too."

"I haven't even seen an alligator snapper before, except in books. Do you think there could be one in this area of Texas?"

"I don't see why not. Alligators live right back up in the Dickinson Bayou and I don't know why alligator snapping turtles don't live around here too."

I got excited and thought about seeing one of those big turtles up close. Alligator snapping turtles were the largest North American turtles and they were also elusive and one of the rarest. Mr. Kimmings could see what I was thinking and asked, "Well? Do you want to come along and help me with the turtle line and maybe catch some catfish?"

I almost turned and ran home to shout at my mom and let her know where I was going before I replied, "You bet! Let me get some better fishing clothes on. Be right back!"

When we got the truck on the road Mr. Kimmings asked me, "How is Rae doing? I mean she is very distant since the car accident and the loss of her friends."

I replied, quietly, "I really don't know. I haven't talked with her. She seems more alone than ever. Do you think I should approach her?"

Mr. Kimmings brow furrowed down and he was quiet for quite a long time. We drove along the shell road, leaving behind a ten-foot high swirling cloud of white dust. I looked at the tallow trees dotting the cow pastures along the sides of the road. He finally sighed and said, "She'll have to work it out. There really isn't much we can do...I mean we can't talk about it and make it better. Rae is a different kind of girl. She has always been...I mean...well; it's hard to explain. Rae thinks too much or maybe she just likes being inside her own mind; it's difficult to understand. I'm her father but I feel I barely know her, you know? She has always solved everything herself. If you try to get too close to Rae she always pulls away. She likes to run from everything. All I can say is try to be her friend. She needs friends. She has never really had any friends that were very close to her, she doesn't allow it, Leslie and Jade were her friends but they never really knew the real Rae, the person inside her."

I understood exactly what he was saying and nodded, saying, "I have always been loyal to Rae. I like her and like being her friend. I have always known to respect her distance. Being Rae's friend isn't easy, you have to know her boundaries and even then you try to approach her with caution until you are sure of her how she feels."

Mr. Kimmings finally laughed loudly, and clapped me on the shoulder, hard, saying, "You got it, boy! Now, that's my daughter! That's Rae! You have her figured out better than I do! Okay now! Let's catch some snapping turtles!"

At the canal we unloaded all the fishing gear and climbed the steep bank through blackberry sticker vines and bull nettles. I looked down from the high bank to the edge of the chocolate water and saw about four lines stretched tightly into the water, anchored to the bank with wooden stakes. Mr. Kimmings carried two fishing poles and some old cow feed sacks, along with a small tackle box. I carried two buckets and another tackle box. We started down the steep bank towards the water and I jumped a little, startled by a loud croak as a huge bullfrog, the size of a chicken, jumped into the canal with a loud splash. Mr. Kimmings snapped his fingers saying, softly, "I wish I would've noticed that big frog before he jumped. Frog legs taste almost as good as turtle soup. Maybe one night soon you and me should come down here and hunt bullfrogs."

I said, "Sure, anytime."

We reached the water's edge and put down the things we were carrying. Mr. Kimmings grabbed the first tight line in the water and said, "Here we go. Let's see if we got any turtles?"

I stood next to him and whispered, "The line is sure tight."

He smiled as he slowly pulled more string from the water, "We have something big on this line."

I saw the first drop hook line come into view and then the water splashed violently as a big bullhead catfish squirmed on the first hook. Mr. Kimmings pulled the fish off the hook and dropped it into the bucket, only half filled with water. He said as he dropped the catfish in the bucket, "I thought at first that it was a madtom catfish instead of a black bullhead. You ever caught a madtom?"

I said, "Nope, but I heard they are poisonous."

"Well, a madtom looks like a bullhead but they have a poison spine on their back and if they stick you it is a very painful sting. Not as bad as a stingray or jellyfish but it hurts like hell anyway. A bullhead will stick you too but it doesn't have any venom in its pectoral spike."

The bullhead catfish was about as long as my forearm, from my elbow to my hand. The second drop hook came out of the water with nothing attached and the bait was gone. The third drop hook was tight and something pulled hard against Mr. Kimmings. He pulled the line in and a common snapping turtle about the size of a frying pan struggled on the hook. Grabbing a pair of needle-nose pliers from his back pocket, Mr. Kimmings worked the hook out of the snapping turtles beak and then grabbed the turtle by its long tail and dropped it in the other bucket. He looked at me and said, "That's one! He's not that big but big enough."

The next two hooks on that line didn't have any bait or a catch on them. Mr. Kimmings rolled the fishing line up and put it in the tackle box. He looked up from the tackle box and said, "Let's check the next one and hope for better luck."

The next two lines produced more turtles. From the other lines three more mid-size snapping turtles were added to the bucket and a channel catfish, larger that the bullhead catfish. We also caught a spotted gar about a foot long but released it back into the water. A gar is a prehistoric fish that sort of resembles a barracuda with a long alligator snout filled with sharp pointed teeth. Mr. Kimmings cut the hook with wire cutters, saying, "It's no use trying to get this hook out of the gars mouth because I am not risking getting one of my fingers cut off by those millions of sharp teeth. It's a wonder the gar didn't cut the line with those teeth. It's hard to catch a gar on a line because they always seem to cut it. Besides that, gars ain't good for eating anyway. I never heard of anybody eating any kind of gar."

I watched the gar roll on the surface slowly and then shoot quickly underwater, disappearing from our view. I said, "Mr. Kimmings, my dad said that people over in Rosharon, over past Alvin, eat gar. We used to go fishing over there in those lakes off the Brazos River. They were full of gar and alligators. There was even a sign that said, 'NO FROG OR ALLIGATOR HUNTING.' Well, we were fishing for crappie and bluegill sun perch when we saw this black family fishing for gar. We talked to them and they had about six dead alligator gars packed up in their station wagon. My dad told me they were going to bar-b-que them."

Mr. Kimmings scratched his head and replied, "Well, I guess there is always somebody that will eat what others won't. Gar-eaters, I guess that's as gross to me as Japanese people eating slimy eels and raw fish. They even have people somewhere in the Middle East that eat bugs. They probably think I'm crazy for eating dead snapping turtles."

I started laughing and he started laughing and finally we just laughed and sat down on the tall reeds that grew on the canals edge. Mr. Kimmings sat there and stop chuckling and picked a tall reed from the ground. He swished it back and forth, making a cool air sound like arrows shot from bows in a movie. I looked down the canal. The water was about thirty yards across and half a mile to the next big culvert. There wasn't any wind blowing and the water was calm. I could see silver fish jumping about every minute or so, mullet, the trash fish of the south. I was told once, and I don't know if it is true or not, that mullet eat mud. How a fish could live by eating mud I don't know but I always remembered that somebody told me that. I do know you can't ever catch a mullet on a lure with a fishing pole, unless maybe your hook actually gets caught in their gills as it is pulled across a school of them. I have always thought that they look like flying fish and they do like to jump out of the water all the time. Actually mullet aren't even related to flying fish as I found out later in life but I still think they could be their cousin's, way back in the family fish tree.

We got up and Mr. Kimmings asked, "You want to pull in the last line for me?"

I smiled and got excited, "Sure, great!"

I bent down and took the line in my hands, pulling slowly on the tight string extending out into the dark murky water of the canal. My imagination ran wild while I pulled, feeling resistance from whatever was on the line down in the water. I imagined that I had hooked into a giant prehistoric sturgeon with curving dragon fins all over its heavily scaled body. The first drop line came out of the water and the line was broken, the hook was gone. I felt a tremendous tightness in the line and it was tough to pull on it. The line shimmered and went back and forth in the water. We had something big fighting on the other end somewhere in that chocolate water. The next drop line came up and another bullhead catfish, smaller this time, twisted on the hook, its gills pumping for air as Mr. Kimmings quickly reached out and let the smaller fish drop back into the water. He nudged me and said, "We'll come back next year and catch him again. Keep on pulling, we got something big hanging on our hook down there!"

The line was so tight I thought it would break at any minute. I tugged as hard as I could and I thought I was going to have to ask Mr. Kimmings to help me with it. Suddenly the water erupted with a violent splash. The water at the canals edge exploded as the next drop line came out into view. I fell backwards, startled by the splashing. I held onto the line and it came even farther out of the water. Mr. Kimmings shouted, "Hang on! Hang on! We got us one! We got an alligator snapper! We got a big one! Don't let him get away! Hang on boy! Don't let him break the line!"

That was when I could see the huge turtle on the hook. I had never seen such an immense turtle except for sea turtles down in Galveston at the Sea Arama Marine Park. This huge alligator snapping turtle thrashed and pulled on our hook like Godzilla of the deep. Mr. Kimmings shouted, "I bet he weighs a hundred pounds, at least! Hang on boy!"

He reached over and we both pulled as hard as we could. I could see the silver hook sticking in the curved beak of the big turtles mouth. The snapper's head was as big as a cantaloupe but his giant shell looked more like a gladiator's shield. The big turtle swished his long alligator tail back and forth like a powerful whip as he dug his clawed feet into the mud trying to move backwards away from the shore. We were in a fight and I shouted while Mr. Kimmings grunted and pulled. The snapper splashed water all over us. The struggle got so loud roseate spoonbills and white herons took flight a hundred yards away.

Suddenly the big turtle lunged forward and snapped its sharp beak shut. I saw the line go into its mouth. We pulled backwards with a surge as the turtle came partially out of the water and I thought we had him then. Just as we pulled the huge snapper halfway onto the shore the line was cut in two by its sharp beak. Mr. Kimmings and I fell backwards onto the mud and reeds. The giant alligator snapping turtle seemed just as surprised as we were. The snapper waited motionless and watched us with dark round eyes as it tried to comprehend that it was free. It seemed like we stared at each other for minutes, me breathing hard and the turtle deciding what to do next. The actual episode of instant freedom only lasted seconds. The turtle whirled like a fast armored tractor with blades cutting hay and with a final loud splash, disappeared back into the dark water of the canal. The last thing I saw was the scaly long alligator tail swishing under.

Mr. Kimmings looked at me and laughed, "Well at least we both saw how big it was. If I tried to describe it to anyone, nobody would believe me. That was the biggest turtle I almost caught. Isn't it always the biggest ones that get away?"

We were muddy and wet but the rest of the day turned out great. We caught a few more catfish, four common snapping turtles and even one red-eared turtle. After we checked all the lines we used our poles and fished for about an hour. I caught a few perch and a small catfish and Mr. Kimmings caught a big carp, which he let go. We took our catch and drove home, tired, but exhilarated. I kept thinking about the struggle with the giant alligator snapping turtle. The more I tried to remember how big the turtle was the bigger it got. I never saw an alligator snapping turtle in Santa Fe, Texas again but I did get to see one in the zoo in Houston. The snapper in the zoo didn't seem as big or fierce and just kind of floated in the water like a big rock. Our snapper in the canal was a monster and in the imagination of my memory it was massive and dangerous and more powerful than a crocodile. We used to swim in the ditches after a heavy rain and we swam in the farm ponds and some of the canals but we never swam in the canal with the giant snapper. Just knowing that such a scary creature with spikes on its tail, a sharp forceful beak, and an armored back was swimming below the dark water was enough to keep me out of that canal.

"...BUT I LIKED THE PLACE BECAUSE IT WAS A FROG PARADISE."

The next afternoon Mr. Kimmings was outside under the shade tree in his front yard. Mrs. Kimmings was sitting on the porch painting on little canvases. She was an artist in her free time. She liked to create tiny little paintings of flowers and birds. Her little paintings reminded me of postage stamps. I always thought she was the person who painted the flowers and birds on the little stamps. Rae was sitting farther away from them under another tree. She was sitting on the grass with a book in her lap. Mr. Kimmings was smoking a pipe and was drinking from a big glass mug. I didn't want to intrude on them and I put my arm up and waved as I walked past heading down the road. Mr. Kimmings waved back but Mrs. Kimmings was too busy painting and Rae's eyes were down in her book. I walked another fifty yards to where our road intersects with the asphalt blacktop, Shouse Road. I headed north on Shouse in the direction of the canals. I wasn't really going to the canals I was just out enjoying the day and the sunshine. I thought I might go to the water station swamp.

I called it the water station swamp but I guess it was really a place where the county had a machine that had something to do with the water or the electricity. Actually I still don't know what the place was for. A cyclone fence on all four sides encircled the silver-metal-water-station machine. It was in the middle of a pasture at the end of a rutted shell road with weeds down the middle. The road was a dead end and only about fifty yards long. The water station released water out the back from a big open pipe. The excess water poured into a semi-circular area, which we called the water station swamp. The swamp was filled with reeds and slime. It was only about two feet deep in most places, shallower than that in others. I had seen many snakes, crawfish, minnows and other inhabitants of the swamp but I liked the place because it was a frog paradise.

The water station swamp was almost directly across the street from old Mr. Frinton's pink house. I was about to turn down the rutted road leading to the water station swamp when I saw Mr. Frinton out in his yard. He waved at me and hollered, "Hey boy! C'mere a second, give me a hand here, would you please?"

He had a shovel in his hand and was digging a small dead tree out of his yard. He asked, "Would you mind helping me out a little? I can't get this root up without letting go of the tree. I been working on this all morning, trying to figure out how to pull and cut at the same time. Here, take this hatchet and chop the roots when I pull the tree back up with the shovel."

He handed me a rusty old hand hatchet with electrical tape on the handle. I thought the hatchet head might fly off the handle if I chopped too hard. Mr. Frinton had on his old straw cowboy hat pulled down low over his ancient eyes and he was wearing his familiar overalls. He didn't have his converse tennis shoes on though. I guess he figured he needed work boots for tree removing. I turned my baseball cap around backwards and knelt down to get a good swing at the tree roots with the rusty hatchet. As Mr. Frinton pulled the tree back, exposing the roots, I chopped and chopped. We kept angling the tree until I had chopped all the roots in a circle around the base of the tree. Mr. Frinton stepped back and wiped his wrinkled brow with a scarf, which he tucked in the band of his straw cowboy hat. The tree was free of its roots. Mr. Frinton said, "Thanks, now if you could help me pull it out of the ground I would appreciate it."

We both grabbed the small tree and pulled and dragged it out of the hole. I sat down as I pulled the heavy tree out and Mr. Frinton's dog, a fat mutt resembling a collie-boxer cross, began licking my face. I nudged the dog away from my face and Mr. Frinton laughed, "That Columbus likes you I think!"

I replied, getting up off the ground, "Yeah, it seems dogs always want to lick me in the face. Why is he named Columbus? After the guy who discovered America?"

Mr. Frinton, chuckling, said, "Nope. People always say that, though. Actually I know people think Columbus discovered America but it just ain't true! The Vikings, the Norsemen, really discovered America. I know what they are teaching you young kids in school. They tell you the story of how Columbus said the world was round when everybody else said the world was flat. So Columbus, in 1492, takes three ships, the Nina, the Pinta, and the Santa Maria, and sails off the flat earth. He sailed across the Atlantic Ocean and discovered the New World. Big Deal! Way before that the Vikings from Norway sailed on their ships to North America. Not the Minnesota Vikings either! The Vikings from Norway had already discovered Iceland and Greenland. Leif Erickson borrowed a Viking long ship and set sail from there to North America, discovering Newfoundland and Canada. This was in 1001, 491 years before Columbus was to land on American shores! Now that is the real history. See how history gets messed up? Just look at the fact that the real Vikings did not wear helmets with horns on them. I think Hollywood created that false image of them and it stuck! Anyway, my dog, Columbus did not get his name from Mr. Columbus, the world traveler. He got his name cuz' that's where I got him. My brother lives over there in Columbus, Texas. He had some pups and gave me the pick of the litter. So I named him Columbus after the place where he was born."

I should have known Mr. Frinton would have a long story to go along with why his dog was named Columbus. Mr. Frinton continued, "go sit on the porch in the shade and I'll get us some iced tea."

I stuck the hatchet in the ground and followed the old man to his porch. I sat in a wicker chair while he went inside to fetch the iced tea. Columbus tried to lick my hands but I pushed him away and he went and stretched out beneath Mr. Frinton's rocking chair. The small dead tree was lying on its side in the yard and a mockingbird flew down and landed on its branches. The gray and white bird began a raucous shrill singing of at least ten different birdcalls. Mr. Frinton soon returned with two glass mugs of cold iced tea. I said, "Thank you," and gulped half of my glass down. He plopped down heavily in his rocking chair and took a swig of his drink. I could tell that he had another story coming on but I was trapped here until I finished my tea and he finished talking. I looked across his yard at the water station swamp. It was only about a hundred yards away but with Mr. Frinton's stories it might as well have been fifty miles away.

He looked me in the eye and said, in his raspy voice, "I really appreciate you helping me with that tree. I would still be out there in the hot sun trying to figure out how to get it out of the ground."

He dug around in his overall chest pocket and pulled

out two quarters, saying, "It ain't much but take this and buy yourself a Coca-cola."

I tried to protest but he continued, "Don't even try it boy, go on and take the coins, you earned it. A man does a good job a man needs to get paid. Someday you might need help with something and you'll remember to appreciate where that help comes from."

I took the two coins and put them in my pocket, saying, "Thanks, Mr. Frinton."

He chuckled a bit and took another drink of iced tea. It was quiet on the porch except for the singing of the mockingbird and the sound of the ice in our glasses clinking when we took drinks. Mr. Frinton raised an eyebrow and said, "I remember another time like this many, many years ago. When I was a young man I was in the war. We had been fighting all week long. I don't know how any of the bullets didn't hit me, I guess I was a lucky soldier. We had made our way to a small town and I remember drinking tea with a young German boy on a concrete porch. I couldn't understand his language and he couldn't understand mine but we both enjoyed the tea and the reprieve from the war. I remember being hot and tired that day too but I didn't have a cowboy hat on, I had a heavy steel army helmet on my head. I got to keep that helmet after the war. I got it inside with a bonsai tree growing out of it. That helmet makes a good planter."

I tried to imagine Mr. Frinton as a young army man wearing a green uniform and a metal helmet. It wasn't an easy image to come up with since I had only known Mr. Frinton as this old man, probably the oldest man in all of Santa Fe. He looked at me with his tired old eyes and continued, "The war was hard on me. I still remember how many of my friends were killed in the mud and the ditches. I came home and they gave me a few medals but I put the medals in the ground with my friends. I was a young man when I went off to war. I had watched my true love die beneath a tree so I left and went to fight. I came home an old man. I was never young again and I never found love again. I don't think I could ever get close enough to life to let love find me. You, young man, if you should find true love, do not let it get away. You should hold onto your youth and grip tightly to love when you find it. Yes, boy, learn from me, an old man with many regrets. Sometimes I think I am immortal, that I will live forever, but to live forever without love is not a good life. I would rather have a short glimpse of true love and die young than an eternity of immortal life without love. Thank you for helping me today. I'm going in now. I am tired."

Mr. Frinton walked slowly in his pink house and I put my empty glass of iced tea on the porch table. I thought I saw a tear forming in his eye as he got up to go inside. I stepped off his porch and the mockingbird suddenly flew from the dead uprooted tree. I left Mr. Frinton's house and walked across the street to the water station swamp.

The swamp was a noisy place. Frog paradise. The many frogs and crickets inhabiting the place sang constantly, almost like nature's full symphony orchestra. There were many species of frogs here but not any of the giant southern bullfrog. Bullfrogs liked more water, deeper water, like the canals and the farm ponds. Here in the tiny swamp there were plenty of cricket frogs, chorus frogs, toads, pickerel frogs, and the bigger leopard frogs. Having so many species of frogs here in such a small area made it a frog paradise for me and for them. The best thing about so many frogs meant that the water was full of thousands of different kinds of tadpoles. I wasn't out here today to catch any of the tadpoles. I just wanted to be away from the house. I climbed up on the large pipe that expelled water into the swamp and watched dragonflies of all colors flying about the reeds. There were many types of damselflies along with the hundreds of dragonflies. Watching the flying antics of so many colored insects like dragonflies and damselflies I imagined that this was a miniature world and the flying insects were tiny multi-colored dragons soaring over their domain. I sat up on that pipe and fell asleep dreaming of riding on the backs of damselfly dragons.

"...BASEBALL WAS TOO BORING FOR US."

A week later and I hadn't seen Rae at all until I went to Runge Park with Kenny Bulbear to play sandlot football. We liked to get games of tackle-no-pads football together out in the outfield of the baseball fields because the grass was soft and green, excellent for getting tackled. We always played football because baseball was too boring for us. There were not enough violent collisions and strategy in boring baseball. When we got through playing football I walked across the road to the water pipe by the white park building for a drink. That's when I saw Rae. She was sitting on a picnic table under a big pecan tree. I stopped walking and just stared. She hadn't seen me and then I saw that she wasn't alone. I recognized whom she was talking to. Sharleen Little was sitting on the side of the table across from Rae. I had heard the rumors like everyone else but I had never seen anything to substantiate them. Rae and Sharleen, together in that way? I didn't think so. Sharleen had been her friend just like Jade and Leslie. Sharleen was probably helping Rae deal with her grief. I quit staring because I felt like I was intruding and began walking back to the field. I felt funny about seeing Rae and Sharleen talking under that pecan tree. I looked back once and saw Sharleen put her hand on Rae's shoulder and I could tell that Rae was crying. I knew then that the rumors were not true. Rae was hurting and Sharleen was a good friend trying to ease her pain. I wanted Rae to snap out of it and if Sharleen could help then that was good.

That night I had a terrible dream and I woke up troubled. I snuck a big glass of milk out of the icebox. I drank it out of my favorite blue metal glass. Cold milk always tastes better when you drink it out of metal glasses. I thought about the dream that woke me up and it wasn't as bad as the one by the ocean but it still scared me. The dream had me dancing with Rae and when I was going to kiss her I saw that her face was Sharleen Little's.

A couple of days later I heard a knock on the front door. My bedroom is right next to the front door because nobody ever comes in that way. The entire neighborhood and everybody we know always enters our house through the door in between the kitchen and the garage. The knock startled me also because nobody ever knocks in our neighborhood. Back then in rural Santa Fe I think most neighborhoods had an open door policy, at least ours did. Nobody ever knocked we just popped in everybody's house. It is not like that anymore. We live in a different world. I jumped up from my chair where I had been listening to record albums of early Genesis and Sly and the Family Stone.

I was the only one home because everyone had gone grocery shopping in Texas City. I opened the door and was surprised to see Rae standing outside on the porch. I should have known it wasn't a stranger in the neighborhood because the dogs didn't bark. The last time some strangers came to our neighborhood they were Jehovah's Witnesses and our dog Bandit bit the man in the butt. Then he hollered and Bandit bit him on the ankle. He ran down the road and dropped a bunch of those pamphlets about Revelations and the end of the world.

Rae was like a golden light shining on the porch. She was smiling, which was rare for her these days. I stood there and stared at her like she was an animal in the zoo or something.

My mouth was open and my eyes took her in as if she was a special scenic overlook. Rae was wearing white shorts, sandals and a yellow tube top. Her blonde hair shimmered like the water down at the lake when the evening sun painted it gold. I stood there too long staring and she said, "Hi, do you want me to stand out here? Are you coming out or am I coming in?"

I stuttered, snapping out of my hallucinatory daze, "Uh, sure. I mean yes. I mean, hey Rae, come on in."

All this time I had known her and this was the first time Rae had ever entered my house. Every other kid in the neighborhood had practically lived at our house. Rae was the only one that kept her distance from everybody. She was the unicorn among the horses. The horses always herd together but the unicorn hides in solitary and secrecy. I held open the door and she entered slowly. The hallway led to the living room but my bedroom door was closer so we just went into my bedroom. She sat in my big chair and I sat on the edge of my bed. The Genesis record was ending on my stereo and another Genesis record was about to drop onto the turntable and began. I turned the volume down and asked, "Rae, how are you? I haven't seen much of you lately. What brings you by here?"

She smiled at me strangely and then a peculiar sadness swept into her beautiful eyes. The transformation was like watching storm clouds from the Gulf of Mexico rumble and then suddenly cover the sun. The sunny day would be gone instantly and wind would blow through your hair and the world would become a gray place, waiting on the coming rain. It was times like that when I would swear I could see the Wicked Witch of the West riding her broom high among the thunderclouds leaving behind a trail of black smoke, saying, "Surrender Dorothy."

Rae fidgeted in the chair, I watched her eyes but I was

distracted as I looked at her tanned pretty legs. She spoke, in a quiet whisper, "I'm thinking of leaving here, Santa Fe. It isn't my kind of place. This town, these people, they are so closed-minded. They are too judgmental and I don't fit in. I don't really know where I should go, maybe California, maybe Florida, maybe Montana where there is nothing but sky and land, somewhere different, away from redneck cow-town U.S.A."

I was stunned. I didn't like what she had to say. I asked her, "Why? It can't be that bad. Come on, Rae. How will you do something like that? You are going to just quit school and leave. How will you make any money? What are you planning on doing, living under some Hollywood freeway? Think about your dad. He is a great guy."

I watched her eyes and saw that the sadness filled them like a flooded reservoir. She almost started to cry but somehow her incredible strength of character stopped the tears. She barely let her eyes get moist and not one teardrop fell on her smooth cheeks. I could see her inner struggle with pain and I knew that all of it did not come from the death of her friends. There were many more circumstances that churned inside of this beautiful mysterious girl. I doubted she would ever share her secret pain with me but I knew she needed a friend right now. I don't think I have ever known a person more alone on the planet than Rae. To this day I still have never met anyone as secret or as sad as the girl who sat one day in my bedroom. She sat in the same big chair that I sat in when I listened to records and did pencil drawings of warriors and creatures, animals and maidens. Rae tossed strands of her long blonde hair back over her shoulders and said, "Yes, my dad means well. He just doesn't understand and he never will. His world is not my world. I don't know why or how it happened but we are too different from each other. I am too different from this world here."

I held up my hand, "Wait, I am different too. I don't think I fit in with all these cowboys and farmers."

She almost laughed, "Yes you are different. That's why I like you so much. You are not like most people here or for that matter, anywhere. But you do fit in. You are a country boy, whether you try not to be doesn't matter, it is part of you. I see in you, the artist, the creative person but I also see the love of a small town and animals. You do belong, way more that I ever will."

I didn't think she was right at the time but now in retrospect she had me pegged perfectly. I tried to argue with her but it did not do any good. Rae sat there in her sadness and depression and told me the truth of things from her perspective. I respected her for her honesty. I watched her pretty face and the way she barely moved in the chair. Rae sat there so still you would hardly know that she was communicating with anyone, especially since her voice was soft and gentle like a floating feather falling out of a cottonwood tree. She said, "Santa Fe is not for me, no matter how much my dad thinks I should live here."

I saw Rae sitting there, so sad yet so beautiful, in my room and I wanted to kiss her. I wanted to hug her and make her smile but more than that I was almost overpowered with the urge to kiss her. I didn't even know how to begin to approach her. I sat there staring at her as she spoke and I noticed that long strands of her hair on the sides of her face seemed to be floating, almost dancing upwards as if she sat in front of an oscillating fan. I was witness to more of the mystery of Rae. There was no fan, no breeze in my room and yet long strands of her grown-out bangs waved upwards and moved like crepe-paper streamers on the Little League floats driving down Hwy 6 opening day of baseball season. In that moment I remembered how she seemed to make a honey bee fly around just by a small movement of her finger. My room seemed suddenly filled with the mystery of this unique, inimitable young girl. Rae was a teenager on the outside but she was ancient and wise within. I realized now why I always seemed intimidated by her. I was like a child compared to Rae's magical insightfulness. She was many immeasurable years beyond my maturity. Rae was almost supernatural to me, a legend in my mind. I was actually in awe and even a little afraid of her.

I watched her stray bangs of hair dance and I looked at the glitter in her eyes that seemed to be caught like flecks of gold in a cavern's walls. She said, "Will you help me leave?"

With her words the spell was broken and I had lost my momentum. I could not make a move to embrace or kiss her now. I didn't want Rae to leave but somehow she controlled my emotions and I could not refuse her. It wasn't magic that moved my heart but it felt like it. I would have fought dragons with only a needle for a sword to help Rae. I looked deep into her peculiar eyes and said quietly, "Yes."

She thanked me and left abruptly. I sat in the chair where she had been sitting and I could still smell her in the fabric. I felt her warmth in the chair. I sat there for a long time and just stared into the air of my room not really seeing anything, except inside my mind. I saw Rae in my room. I could see her beautiful eyes looking into mine. I had agreed to help her leave Santa Fe. I had agreed to help her leave from me. I didn't know what love was at that time but now I can see that love had blinded me. I'm sure most people would say it was puppy love or infatuation but whatever the definition it was something magical that had put a ring in my nose and Rae could have led me all around the world with it. The thing is she never knew what feelings lurked deep inside of my heart. I was going to help her leave here and she didn't even know how I truly felt. I thought that maybe if I had enough courage to tell her, just maybe she would stay. I must be stupid to think she would care enough to stay. I would help her leave and then she would be happy. I had promised and I would keep my promise to her.

"...HE HIT ME IN THE FACE SO HARD I FELL BACKWARDS..."

The next day I was up at the Moody Grocery Store on Highway 646 with Skip Howing. We had always gone up to the store to buy lemon-lime flavored Slushes. I still think on a hot Texas day there is nothing that tastes better than a cold lemon-lime Slush. I followed Skip out the glass door of the Moody Grocery Store and in the small shell-dust parking lot was Rae. She was standing next to her bike. I never knew Rae to ride her bike very often but I guess anyone would ride to the Moody Grocery Store for a cold slush on a day as hot as this one. She waved with her left hand and held onto her bike with her right. The sunlight glinted off her long blonde hair like shimmering flashes of chrome. I waved back and Skip said, "Hey Rae! You ride your bike all the way up here for a Slush?"

Before she could reply a beat up 1960 Chevy pickup truck roared into the parking lot stirring up a big cloud of shell dust. The door of the truck opened with a loud groan of rust and metal as out stepped Rory Marks. "Hello, Rae, I haven't seen you in quite awhile. In fact I have been thinking about you and I been missing seeing you around. Why don't you throw your bike in the back of my truck and we'll go for a ride?"

I looked at Rory's smug face and then back at Rae. She parked her bike up next to the grocery store brick wall and walked towards the door. Skip and I had not moved and as she got closer to us she replied in a cold voice, "Rory, please leave me alone."

He laughed, a low chuckle filled with bad intent. Rory, still laughing, said, "Rae, Rae, c'mon hop in with me. What? You want to hang out with these two losers? How about you two losers, ya'll want to go for a ride with me too? Probably be the best ride you will ever take. C'mon Skip let's go do donuts in your dad's rice fields!"

Rae stopped and faced Rory, saying, "Leave them alone Rory Marks! Just leave them alone!"

I couldn't hold back any more and walked up and put my face inches from Rory's and shouted at him, "Get out of here you jerk! Leave us alone! It's your fault Jade and Leslie are gone! Won't you ever learn?"

I saw deep into his eyes and thought I could see fear, but I was wrong I guess, because he hit me in the face so hard I fell backwards and hit my head on the cement sidewalk. Rae jumped past Skip who just stood there staring as I hit the ground. She slapped Rory in the face and he backhanded her hard enough to knock her back. Skip started to say something but Rory took a step towards him and he backed off. I groaned on the sidewalk and sat up holding my head and noticed that my nose was bleeding. Rory shouted at Skip, "You want some too? I didn't think so!"

Rory walked past us and into the store. Skip asked if I was okay as he helped me up. Rae held her face where she had been hit and came to look at me, saying, "I'm sorry. Are you sure you're okay? Maybe you should see a doctor just in case?"

I waved them back, "I'm okay. My head hurts and my nose is bleeding but I think I should have at least hit him once. Let's get out of here before he decides to come out of the store and pick up where he left off."

They all turned when they heard a voice from the corner of the store. The voice said, "You three should have whupped that bad boy's butt. I think maybe he needs a good whuppin' too! He ain't no better than his dad was back in the day. His pappa was a coward and a bully."

It was old Mr. Frinton, standing there, telling us what we should do. I was holding my head and Rae had given me a handkerchief to wipe the blood from my nose. Mr. Frinton shook his head, saying, "Yes, that boy needs a butt whuppin' soon to put him in his place."

I looked at Skip and he was nodding his head in agreement with old man Frinton. Mr. Frinton had faded overalls on and a t-shirt with pieces of straw stuck to it. He dusted me off a bit and put an old wrinkled hand on my shoulder, saying, "You're a good boy. I know your family and I know what you stand for."

He glanced at Skip and continued, "You too, boy. Both of you are good boys and don't need to go around and let some trash talking mockingbird like that kid go a-pickin' on you. If he comes out of that store and so much as starts with his crap again, I think if you two don't go at him I'll step up and knot his head with one of these bony fists of mine! And you too girl, get a few licks in while you're at it. I tell you three; he ain't nothing but a coward and will back down if you would ever just stand up to him together. His father was the same way. He ended up working as a rodeo clown after quitting high school. He wasn't any good at rodeoing or fighting bulls. It is kind of hard to be a rodeo clown if you are yellow inside, scared of bulls. This boy is just like his dad, I can tell, a bully and a coward at heart."

I felt my nose throbbing and I listened to those words about standing together and I remembered something that had happened a few years back in junior high. I think I was in the seventh grade and it was summer time. I was spending the weekend with a friend on the northeast side of Alta Loma, close to Dickinson, Texas. He was the smartest kid in school and was actually younger than I was but had been bumped up a grade because he had so much intelligence. I remember he had already read all the John Norman "Gor" novels by eighth grade, and I never even heard of them much less read them. I finally read them, seven years later in about 1978. He was a chubby guy with pink cheeks and his name was Bernard Tottenhill. He was girl crazy but scared to death of them. I don't think he ever even talked to a girl. He could make straight A's, beat anybody in chess or Risk, and he even tried football but he was too slow and tired all the time. Bernie was a good friend but we didn't live very close to one another so once in a while I would spent the weekend at his house. His mom was always very nice. She baked cookies and brownies and let us drink all the Coca-Cola we wanted.

"...GIANT DINOSAUR T-REX HEADS PUMPED OIL UP AND DOWN..."

That summer day, when I stayed with him, we decided to go exploring out in the pastures directly across from his house. Another boy that lived across the street from him went to school with us and he decided to come along too. His name was Stan Loopner. Stan wasn't really our friend but since he lived across from Bernie we let him tag along. Stan Loopner never really did become good friends with us because later in school he got into too much trouble and eventually had to get married. He vandalized a Dairy Queen by exploding the toilet and flooding the restroom. He also once tied three cats together by their tails and they ran off into the woods. I heard that they had gotten tangled up in a barbwire fence and clawed each other to death. He left high school early and started a roofing business with money he inherited from his father. Bernie, Stan, and I left the road and crawled under a barbwire fence. Stan said that there was a big pond only a couple of miles out, near a stand of tallow trees. We set off for the trees in the distance.

The cow pasture was filled with oil well derricks. Oil well pumps that looked like giant dinosaur T—rex heads pumped oil up and down like greasy seesaws. I always liked to watch those T-rex heads bobbing up and down pumping oil. Bernie was carrying the fishing poles, I had a big bucket and a net and Stan didn't carry anything but he did have a big buck knife in his pocket. It was late in the afternoon and this summer it hadn't rained in almost a month. The weeds were brown and scratchy and the ground looked like a giraffe's hide, with cracks in a reticulated pattern. Hiking across this vast parched cow pasture I felt like I was in the Arizona desert, all I needed to see now was a big Saguaro cactus, or better than that a camel plodding along the horizon. I was excited because during hot summers like this the ponds dried almost up, leaving all kinds of fish and animals stranded in the shallow water. The shallow water that was left in the dried-up ponds always attracted other animals too. With the pond fish crowded into small shallow pools of evaporating water the predators all came to eat. Snakes, raccoons, coyotes, bobcats, and other animals with a fish taste came down to find a snack. I liked the excitement of not knowing what kind of creatures we might stumble upon.

We reached the pond and Stan was right, it was a big one. The summer sun had done the damage and the water was almost gone. The pond was about a hundred yards long and only thirty or so yards wide but it was now dried up, leaving only four shallow pools of water surrounded by thick mud. The mud around each pool was filed with tracks of dozens of animals. I could see many egret and heron tracks dominating the pools. There were also raccoon, opossum, bobcat, coyote, and some larger tracks that I thought might be red wolves. As we stepped out of the cover of the trees a large Great Blue Heron launched itself into the air with a loud flap of huge five-foot wings. I watched the largest bird in Santa Fe, Texas, fly slowly over the trees and out of sight, thinking about how this could have been a prehistoric moment and the heron looked so much like a giant pterosaur flapping over an antediluvian landscape. I heard a Killdeer cry and watched as the little white-bellied bird dragged one wing, feigning injury to lure us away from its nest. Stan and Bernie ignored the birds and walked closer to the biggest pool in the center of the pond.

I heard Bernie yell, "Come here, quick!"

Stan pulled out his knife and walked slowly towards the mud. I ran over to them and saw, near the water, a large gray-black cottonmouth water moccasin. The venomous snake was gorged on fish and its thick body was huge and bloated. This snake was dangerous because it was in no mood to be disturbed. The snake did not want to move or give up its feast. Most snakes would rather escape and slither away quickly when confronted but not this big monster. This snake was too big and too dangerous. This snake thought of itself as "king" of the pond. Stan was a fool if he thought he would get close enough to stab it with the knife. The big heavy snake flicked its forked tongue continuously as if saying, "I see your knife, boy. Why don't you come down here in the mud and play with me?"

I whispered to Stan, "Hey, be careful. Stay away from it."

Stan replied, not even whispering, "I kill snakes all the time, don't worry about me."

I said, "Wait, I got a better idea."

I looked around, put the bucket and the net down, and said, "Keep an eye on him and don't move. He might get an idea to attack or hide in the muddy water. We got to kill him because he isn't going to give up his pool."

I went back into the trees searching for a long heavy stick. The stick had to be long enough and it also had to have a forked piece of branch on it. I found a thick broken branch about ten feet long and I had to break a slender branch from it to make the forked end. I came back along side Stan with his knife and Bernie, still holding the fishing poles. I walked past them and said, "Stay back!"

I had the snake handling experience and I didn't trust

Stan with that crazy look in his eyes, armed with that knife. I also knew Bernie was not going anywhere near a snake. I stepped slowly into the soft mud and cautiously approached the big mud covered cottonmouth water moccasin. The big snake slithered as I moved towards it. The snake turned its body, twisting into a curving series of "s" shapes. It was now facing me with that flicking forked tongue tasting the air. I was about eight feet away when the huge snake opened its mouth and hissed loudly like a hot air balloon losing helium. I could see the stark white inside of the snake's mouth and the two deadly curving fangs, like syringes, filled with venom. There were "s" shapes in the mud all around the shallow pool as the snake had slithered around eating fish. I could see the hundreds of minnows darting in schools in the shallow water. The tiny fish swam back and forth with no escape, trapped in the muddy water hole. I could also see big catfish fins sticking up swimming in the chocolate water. I would have to kill this water moccasin "king" of the pond so we could catch all these fish.

The mud was sucking my shoes down and making it hard for me to move quickly. That's why getting close to this snake was so dangerous. My mobility was limited and the big snake was faster on the mud than on dry ground. The slick mud was like a slide for the sinuous serpent. I got as close as I could without causing the snake to strike, staying just out of his extended range but close enough to try and get my long stick on his body. To kill this snake I would have to get it out of the mud and onto hard dry ground. I had planned to pin it with the forked stick and then toss it onto the dry ground at the pond's edge. Normally I would pin a snake and then work my way with a stick up the long body until I had pinned the head. I would then grab a snake behind the head and capture it. I did not want to try this technique with this very large and dangerous water moccasin. I was breathing hard as I got ready to attack the snake. I would pin it with the long stick and then toss it forward to the hard ground. I would have to move quickly to run to where it would land and pin it to the ground with the stick before it could slither back into the mud and water. Pinned to the hard ground we could kill it with big sticks by pounding its dangerous head.

Stan had already picked up a club as if he knew to be ready but Bernie just watched like a cherub, oblivious of the real danger. I guess he thought he was watching PBS and this was the snake catching show. He still held the fishing poles. Maybe Bernie thought he was going fishing for big black water moccasin. I held the long stick out in front of me and the snake lunged at it, striking with that white mouth and hissing loudly. It struck again and I moved quickly. I thrust the long forked stick out after the snake missed with its strike. The fork of the stick stuck in the mud and covered a coil of the snake about halfway down its fat body. I twisted the stick and picked the writhing snake up in one motion. The hissing seemed to be so loud that it pierced my eardrums. It was like I had a dragon impaled on a long sword and it spat bursts of sound fire towards me, scorching my armor. Adrenalin shot through my body and I instantly swept the snake out of the mud like a slap shot with a hockey stick. I hadn't realized that Stan and Bernie had been moving behind me and Bernie had made his way for a better view right into the direction that I threw the deadly snake. It was moments like this that my mother had nightmares about, wondering what I was doing out in the pastures and the woods.

The wet, muddy snake hit Bernie in the leg and landed between his legs. I was moving towards him as soon as I let the snake fly from the forked stick. Bernie dropped the fishing poles but he didn't move. He looked down at the hissing water moccasin on the ground between his feet, its tail across his right shoe. The snake struck quickly, hitting Bernie's leg. I got there too late and slammed the long stick down on the snake's head just as it prepared to strike again. I pinned the hissing head to the hard dirt. Stan was next to me pounding the snake with the thick club. I yelled at him, "The head! Hit the head! Smash it before it squirms away and bites!"

I held the snake down with the stick and Stan swung the club like Thor with his Thunder Hammer pounding the sky into a storm. I don't know how many times Stan hit that snake but the head had disappeared into the ground. The long thick body still squirmed and coiled, moving like some headless octopus tentacle. I knew it was dead and I said, "Nerves. Nerves make it keep moving. It's dead. Dang that is a big snake."

Then I remembered that it bit Bernie. Bernie looked like he was going to cry. His rosy cheeks were bright red now and the fishing poles were tangled up together. The poles looking like an "x" with strands of spider web spun around entangling them. Bernie sat down and rolled his pants leg up looking for the fang marks. Stan and I bent down and searched for the two tiny punctures. Stan had his knife ready to make a cut so we could try to suck some of the poison out. I looked at Bernie's pants and found the two tiny holes in the material. I said, "Where does it hurt, Bernie?"

He stuttered, "I don't know, it doesn't hurt. I can't feel my legs. Help me, I'm gonna' die. My mom is gonna' kill me. I don't want to die! I can't feel my legs! I can't feel my legs!"

Bernie was starting to hyperventilate. I grabbed him by the shoulders and screamed, "Bernie! Bernie! You ain't bit! You ain't gonna' die! The snake just bit your pants! Quit it! You ain't gonna' die! Tell him Stan!"

We couldn't find any bite marks on his leg. The snake had hit his pants and luckily had not penetrated his skin. Stan slapped Bernie in the face, and yelled at him, "Shut up Bernie! You ain't bit! You got lucky this time! Next time you stay out of the way and leave the snakes up to me! I killed that snake real good. You can't even tell he ever had a head!"

Bernie started crying then. There were lots of tears strolling down his baby face. I felt sorry for him. He couldn't help it. Stan didn't need to slap him so hard. I bet his mother didn't even slap him hard. Knowing his mom, I bet she never even slapped him. We all went over under a shade tree and sat down. Nobody talked for a few minutes. Bernie finally stopped crying and Stan carved a piece of wood with his knife. I tried to untangle the fishing poles but I was about to give up. I guess we each were absorbed in our own space and weren't aware of what was going on around us because something moved down at the end of the pond.

I didn't really see anything move. It was more like I felt something was there. It was like the feeling I would get when Rae did something strange and mysterious. It was something magical like a bee following her finger. We had just killed the water moccasin "king" of the pond and sat quietly under a shade tree. Those are the moments when magic happens. Those moments when you are not imposing on nature but camouflaged as a part of the wilderness. I felt the air get thinner and lighter around me. The tiny hairs on the back of my neck stood up. This moment sort of felt like the moment when the air gets colder and the thunderclouds roll in. Those few minutes before a summer storm comes. It was hot and sunny and there wasn't storm on the horizon. Magic was here in this quiet place, the magic of being in the right place at the right time. I don't know if Bernie or Stan were aware of any of this and I don't think that they were. Stan carved splinters of wood and Bernie was probably thinking about his mother's brownies. I was feeling the first edge of this magic. A feeling crept over me, a feeling of calm and contentment. I felt relaxed and yet on the cusp of something new and profound. I felt like God was looking down and whispering in my ear. I was about to see a magical scene, a secret realm of Mother Nature's world opened up to me.

From the concealment of the trees I looked down the length of the pond. That's when I saw them. This is the only time I have ever seen them and I never saw them again in my life. The animals trotted down to the water's edge and each bent to drink, taking turns. The red wolves were tall and majestic. At first I thought they were coyotes but it didn't take long for me to realize that coyotes were never this big or this powerful. There were five red wolves at the water hole at the far end of the pond. I watched in silence, never taking my eyes from the wolves as they each drank from the pond. The tallest wolf stopped while drinking and looked directly at me. His tall ears stood up and his yellow eyes pierced into mine like hot fires. He had the same unique pools of mystery in his eyes that Rae possessed. The big alpha wolf had water dripping from his snout and I could see his wet, muddy feet as he stood next to the pond. The other wolves looked my way but then went back to their sniffing the air and biting each other in play. The big red wolf bent to drink again, disregarding me. I think he had looked into my eyes and read my soul. He was aware of my intentions and disposition. In that mystical moment the red wolf and I knew each other on a deeper level than reality. He drank his fill and trotted off into the trees followed by the rest of the pack. I watched their swishing tails as they disappeared from view, hidden by the undergrowth and the trees. Now it seemed as if they had never been there.

I looked at Stan and Bernie and back at the spot where the wolves had been. The feeling of magic was gone, only a residue of mystical imprints left on my soul. I would never forget that moment and the wolves that once roamed Santa Fe. Stan and Bernie had never even seen the wolves. Stan had never looked up from his woodcarving and Bernie was still sniffling about almost being bitten by a poisonous snake. I think I had been specially chosen to be a part of that magic by the powers of nature. Too many people in our world are never chosen to experience the mystical significance of nature's secrets. There is a world of concrete and cars that has almost forgotten the secret world of the barn owl and the red wolf, the bobcat and pipistrel bat, the nutria and the alligator snapping turtle. These things can be seen in zoos. We take a few minutes watching them sleep in an enclosure but to experience those red wolves when they were wild and part of the natural terrain, a trotting creature of regal power and cunning roaming the land is to truly know what life forces are generated from the earth and the universe. I looked over at Stan and Bernie and thought about telling them about the red wolves. I looked at them and then I didn't say anything. The moment was only for me, not to be shared. I thought that if I shared the wolves they would lose their magic. I still think about the pack of red wolves and I always wondered what became of them. Santa Fe is more of a spread out metropolis now instead of a wild place. The wolves might still be there hiding in secret pockets of wood and prowling in the shadows at night. I always hope they are still around but my heart knows that more likely they have moved on or been killed, driven into extinction by more roads and concrete.

Bernie stopped sniffling and slapped Stan on the back, saying, "C'mon, Stan, let's catch some fish!"

He jumped up and I stood up too as Stan put up his knife and his woodcarving. I noticed that the piece of wood he had been carving sort of looked like a wolf, but it was probably supposed to be his dog, an elkhound named Sookie. I grabbed the net and handed Stan the bucket, saying, "I saw a big fin in the last pool down there. I don't know if it is a big catfish or what. Let's go get it!"

We caught three large bullhead catfish and one humongous carp. We let the carp go because my dad told me before that you shouldn't eat carp fish. I figured it was because carp fish had poison meat or maybe it was because it would be like eating your giant pet goldfish. With me lugging the bucket filled with the three catfish we gathered our stuff and started the long walk back to Bernie's house. As we neared the oil dinosaurs pumping their long necks Bernie started dancing around like an idiot. I guess he had a fun time catching catfish or maybe he was glad we were almost to his house but anyway he started singing some stupid cartoon theme song, I think it was "Underdog." Bernie was skipping and singing and he sort of trotted towards the oil pumps while Stan and I walked slowly, me, because the bucket was getting heavier and Stan because he was carving again as he walked. Next thing we know Bernie is hollering instead of singing.

The cracked ground around the oil pumps is really just an illusion of solid dried up earth when underneath it is really is a bed of sticky oil muck like a La Brea tar pit. Bernie ran out there across that tar pit thinking he was still on dried pasture dirt. He was up to his knees in a few seconds getting deeper in the pitch, black muck; oil mud quicksand is what I always called it. He had dropped the fishing poles a few yards back and they were covered in oil muck. I never heard of anyone getting sucked all the way under like the quicksand in those

"Tarzan" movies but Bernie was getting sucked into the Santa Fe tar pit and he was scared and hollering like he was going to die. Stan started laughing and I just put the bucket down and yelled at Bernie, "Hold on, you ain't going under. We'll get you out! Stan stop laughing and look for a big long stick so we can get him out of there."

Stan kept laughing and said, "Hey Bernie, you look like a big woolly mammoth stuck in the tar pit!"

Bernie just screamed back, "Help me! I'm stuck! Get me out of here!"

I had to go a long way back to the trees to finally find a broken tree branch long enough to reach Bernie. I carried the long swaying branch back to where Stan was watching Bernie getting stuck deeper in the black muck. I yelled at Bernie, "Grab on to the stick and we'll pull you out!"

I extended the stick to Bernie and I told Stan to grab my ankles as I leaned out across the dried ground. Bernie grabbed onto the long stick and Stan pulled backwards as we slowly dragged Bernie out of the tar pit. Bernie looked back at the black pit and saw the fishing poles out in the muck. He looked at me and said, "What about the poles? We got to get them out. I'll get in trouble if we don't bring the poles back!"

I just shook my head and laughed, "Bernie, Bernie, you are already in trouble. Just take a look down at your clothes. Your momma is going to kill you when she sees your clothes. We can't get those poles and I am not crawling out into the oil mud to get them."

Bernie was covered from his waist down in the thickest slick black oil mud I had ever seen. His clothes were ruined. Bernie's mom would never let him go on an adventure with me ever again. We tried to show her the catfish in the bucket but his mom only saw Bernie's ruined clothes and all the oil mud. She even screamed at him about his ruined shoes, which I didn't know were only a few days old. Stan went home before she started hollering at him but I had to stay and listen. Bernie and I never spent much time together after that day.

A few years later Bernie took up marathon running and lost all his excess weight. He started talking to girls and soon he was dating a cheerleader in high school. We drifted apart and he eventually went off to Harvard or Yale or somewhere like that. Bernie finished college early with honors and I heard that he lives in Canada in a mansion. He became a successful gynecologist and something of an international playboy. I saw him once at a hometown football game and he looked very different than the boy I knew. I wondered if he ever thought about how we saved him from the Santa Fe tar pit. I guess those fishing poles are still out there in that pasture under the earth, sinking deeper by the year. That pasture is probably gone and houses are built on top of the fishing poles.

Stan and I and Bernie had stood together and survived the tar pits and the snake attack. There had been a time that we stood together, even though now we are in different corners of the planet. We acted as one to accomplish something and we succeeded. It took all of us to accomplish something and today, with Rory, was the same situation. Standing together we could triumph and only alone we could each fail. Even if we never saw each other again at least this day we could act as one and stand up together against Rory. I made up my mind as my nose ached and my head throbbed. I looked at Skip and Rae and said, "Let's do it."

Rory opened the door and stepped out of the store right as my right fist slammed into his cheek. Skip was next to me and hit Rory in the stomach as hard as he could. Rory fell down on his knees and I hit him again in the back as Skip took another swing, connecting in his ribs. We stepped back as Rory breathed hard and he said, "You two are gonna' die."

That's all he got to say because Rae stepped up and slapped him as hard as she could in the face and his head popped back. He started to get up and go after her but I swung at his face with my fist and hit him square in the neck instead. Skip was already attacking and hit him in the stomach two more times. Rory went down choking and holding his neck. I stood over him with Skip on one side and Rae on the other. Mr. Frinton was clapping behind us. I clenched my teeth and said to Rory, his face bleeding as he sucked air, "Stay away from us. If you want more of this we can give it to you. Next time we won't be so nice. Get up and get out of here before you get some more."

Skip, chimed in, "Yeah, and remember, I'll kick your butt worse next time, go on!"

Rory slowly got up and hobbled to his truck and drove off, squealing his tires. Mr. Frinton was smiling as we looked back at him still clapping. I wasn't smiling but I felt good about myself for finally standing up to Rory Marks. We all had and Skip seemed to be taller than before. Rae smiled at me and I felt that proud smile go all the way into my skin and saturate my soul. To get a true smile from Rae like that was worth almost anything to me. I was basking in her smile and then I remembered I was supposed to help her leave here. Mr. Frinton put his hand on my shoulder and said, "I am proud of you son. Teaching someone a lesson isn't always easy but the hard part is learning it. Because of what happened to that Marks kid here today maybe his life will turn out better than his rodeo clown father's. I wouldn't be surprised to see him straighten up and become a better person. What ya'll did, by standing up to him, was teach him a lesson in humility, something which he probably never experienced. Maybe he will think about this day and the next time he is put in a situation where he is the bully he might actually right his own wrong."

He paused, with his old hand still on my shoulder and he looked at each of us in turn, as he said, "You did right and it might change a person's life. Be proud of yourselves."

Mr. Frinton smiled like an old snapping turtle popping his head out of the canal water and then he turned and went inside the store. Rae touched my face and smiled, saying, "Thanks and remember, you promised."

She followed Mr. Frinton into the store and Skip and I weren't far behind. We all gulped our cold drinks and sweated outside the store. The taste of a good cold slush from the Moody Grocery Store with friends in the hot Texas sun was one of life's better moments back then. That was a good day. It was one of the last good days with Rae Kimmings in Santa Fe, Texas.

"…I WITNESSED THE BLACK WIND."

Later that day when I was alone down by the rice canals north of my house I witnessed the black wind. I called it the black wind because I had never seen such a thing before. I looked down Shouse Road and saw a black moving cloud wavering like a flock of cowbirds in flight. At first I thought it was a massive flock of low flying blackbirds. I knew it wasn't smoke because it wasn't coming from the ground, just wavering and moving in the air like a dark imposing cloud. As it neared me I didn't feel fear, only wonder and awe. That's when I saw the first few flying near my face, my hands, and my body. It was the largest mass of love bugs flying I had ever seen. It made me remember one time when my Paw Paw was driving on Highway 2004 south and I was in the front seat holding his small radio listening to the Astros baseball game. We had just passed Chocolate Bayou when little black bugs began hitting the windshield and splattering. My Paw Paw had to slow down because they were so many of them it was like black rain and the windshield wipers only made a mess. We had to finally stop and my Paw Paw poured a jug of water he kept in the back seat on the windshield to clean off the hundreds of dead love bugs.

I didn't know the real name of love bugs but I think they are related to lightning bugs. They resemble each other except that love bugs are black with a red spot on them and lightning bugs are yellow with black stripes. Love bugs got their name because they mate in flight and fly attached together like they are "in love." Suddenly they sky was covered as the immense horde of love bugs flew all around me. I could feel them landing all over my clothes and my skin. The tiny black-winged insects flew in the thousands around me. Their soft bodies tickled my skin like small feathers. I had to shut my eyes to keep the little insects from flying into them. I was surrounded by the swarm of love bugs for many minutes and it felt like a lot longer than that but I felt special, like they had chosen me to fly around. I felt like they knew I was not dangerous or afraid and they all flew closer to bless me with their "love." I always remembered that day and thought of it as a special omen, a true gift from nature. The love bugs had given me the emotional power to love more deeply than most humans and I have always cherished their gift.

That evening my mom told me that their had been several car wrecks that day in Alta Loma due to a freak swarm of insects on the roadways. Nobody had been hurt but Al Simpson at the Farmer Insurance place wasn't very happy with all the accident claims. That's the last time I ever heard of cars wrecking because of insect swarms. I still see love bugs swarms but they never approach the size of that massive grouping that touched and surrounded me that day. I never kill love bugs willfully and I always try to help them on their way if they need it. The love bug's numbers are dwindling these days and I miss their clouds of "love." Thinking of the love bugs and their decline I also think of the other declining species in Galveston County and of how not many people care about their habitat. Every time I turn around more land is cleared, more animals have no place to go. South Texas is sadly lacking in wildlife sanctuaries and parks. This makes me saddened to think that my birthplace is negligent to the lost wild nature of Galveston

County. How many more creatures go the way of the Texas horned lizard? The horny toads are gone and what other species will disappear from here forever?

"SHE SAID, "STARS ARE DISAPPEARING.""

That night I thought back to those days in junior high when I saw the pack of red wolves. Three young boys out in the Texas wilds and all three of us would go in different directions from that day forth. Life was simple back then and I still want things to trickle down to the simplest level these days. There have been times when I wish I could go back and sit at the edge of that pond and just stare at the place where the red wolves drank. The pond is still there but the land around it has acquired a few houses and the woods have been cleared. The red wolves have long vanished as have those places of my youth. I saw a coyote on highway 1764 near the freeway and it looked afraid and lost, as if it couldn't comprehend where it was or how it had gotten there. The woods are gone and the prairies are small, bordered by buildings and fences. The coyote stared into my headlights as if he had no hope and then he turned and trotted off across a deserted parking lot by the Greyhound Dog Track.

That day with Rae and Skip and Mr. Frinton at the Moody Grocery store was a good highlight and made for a good week. Rae and I talked a few times in her yard but she didn't mention my promise again. We sat in lawn chairs on a Thursday night in front of her house and she told me about the stars. She said, "Stars are disappearing."

I just looked at her and drank in her smooth skin, tanned legs and pretty face with those blue-green eyes that flickered like scintillating crystals. I listened to her like she knew everything that I wanted to know. I was staring at her eyes and her straight yellow hair shining in the dim light of dusk approaching full dark. She repeated, nudging me, "Stars are disappearing."

I jerked up, startled by her friendly touch, said, "Stars? They are?"

"Yes," she said, "They are disappearing because of people."

I looked up expecting to see fewer stars than usual. The night sky was as vast as I remembered it, with plenty of stars spread out like a cup of spilled sugar on black velvet. Rae looked up also and continued, "Someday we will see only half of all the stars or maybe not even that many. The lights of cities are so bright that the sky becomes a paler background and we lose sight of many of the stars. Have you ever been to Montana? The sky there has more stars. I heard it once said by my old science teacher that we will lose sight of the stars because of what he called, 'light pollution.' I love the stars and that is why I will never live in a big city."

I didn't know much about astronomy but I did know that out in the woods the stars seemed brighter than on our front porch. I looked back at Rae, and thought about what she wanted to leave in my mind. I could see a tear slowly form at the corner of her eyes. I asked her, "Rae, is that where you want to go? Montana?"

"Someday I want to go to Montana but for now I think I will go to Florida. I have been reading about the Florida Keys. I want to disappear down there near the ocean on those tiny islands that stretch out from the land. I think the Keys are what I have been searching for. It is like they have been calling to my spirit, my soul, pulling me south. I went out to the Galveston beach and felt an inner tug from across the Gulf of Mexico. I stared out over that chocolate ugly beach water of Galveston and envisioned the clear water and white sand of the Florida Keys. The ocean has always called to my heart, not the mountains or the canyons, but the ocean is where I belong."

I reached out and took her hand. She looked deep into my eyes and entwined her delicate fingers in mine. I felt warmth coursing up my arm. I felt almost as if my skin was glowing. Holding hands with Rae was like feeling on the inside the way Snoopy dances when Schroeder plays the piano on Peanuts. I didn't speak for several minutes. We sat there looking up at the vast trillions of stars, holding hands, and silently enjoyed our companionship, our unique friendship. I finally looked back at Rae, studying her profile. Her smooth skin in the dim light of the night seemed to be painted with a satin sheen. I observed how long and thick her eyelashes were as I watched her eyes illuminate my heart like mysterious crystals. I said, in a whisper so as not to disturb the moment, "Rae. Rae, do you really have to leave? I want you to stay."

Her eyebrows knitted and lines of worry and concern creased her pretty face and she replied quietly, "Yes. I will miss you. I need to go soon. I have made my decision and I can't let anything stop me. I know I would regret it if I didn't leave. If I stayed here my life would be unfair to my heart and my dreams. I would regret not going and grudge you or anyone else that I stayed for. As much as we share, and I hold you very close, I still must follow my own way. My destiny lies elsewhere, not here, not in Santa Fe, not with my Dad, not in Texas. I cannot wait much longer to begin my journey. When I was out in the pastures I knew you watched from on top of the barn. I have known how you feel about me. Your heart is precious and I know what I mean to you. You are special to me too. We are young and life is like the stars, trillions of points of light calling us to different destinations, different futures. Mine lies far away from here. You should follow where your soul leads."

She kissed me, softly and slowly. Her delicate kiss took me by surprise. I kissed her, drinking her in like she was the last drop of water in a desert. She pulled back too soon and it felt like I had dreamt that her lips had touched mine. I could not speak. I could only think about her leaving. She squeezed my hand and stood up. I remained sitting and she reached down and touched my cheek gently, saying, "Goodnight."

Rae walked away closing the door of her house quietly. I sat in the yard looking up at the stars for another hour. I slept deeply that night and had a dream about Rae. I dreamt that she was living in a small cottage on stilts near the ocean in the Florida Keys. I could see her lying in a hammock suspended between two palm trees on a white sandy beach. In my dream I was wearing cut-off blue-jean shorts, no shirt, and no shoes, walking along the hot sand while fiddler crabs scrambled sideways to get out of my way. I walked right up to Rae and she held her hand out to me. I reached for her hand but before I could grab it a honeybee flew between us. I watched transfixed as she guided the honeybee in circles with just her little pinky finger. She made the tiny bee fly in loop-de-loops, and upside down, and figure eights. Whatever motion she made with her finger the tiny honeybee followed her instructions. She made the bee do aerial trick after trick until finally she pointed off towards the surf. The honeybee alighted on the end of her finger and then shot off into the horizon. Rae was smiling bigger and more genuine than I have ever seen her. The surroundings had enabled her to become more beautiful and exciting. I was mesmerized and stared at her like she was some enchanted island goddess, queen of all she could see. As if to bring to life my thoughts, brightly colored macaws, blue and yellow, red and gold, flew towards us and landed on the hammock and in the palm trees. The large birds flew noiselessly, followed by other birds landing all around us. Ruby throated hummingbirds darting in the air like glittering crystals of green and red, magnificent white pelicans glided onto the beach and landed at the edge of the blue-green surf like albino pterodactyls, and pink flamingos flapped their black tipped wings and landed in the hundreds all along the beach. Warblers, finches, and songbirds of a myriad of colors filled the air and the trees. The birds cacophony of color boggled the senses but the ornithologist's paradise was silent, not a single bird made a chirp or a squawk.

Rae reclined and smiled like this was the greatest present she had ever received. I stood there, stunned by such immense magic and mystery. Rae spread her arms and the birds along the beach parted to either side to allow us a clear view of the water. The white crested waves broke with foam and the shades of blue and green in the clear water was like phosphorescent paint on a stark painter's canvas. So much pure color and the awesome power of nature pulled a trigger in my mind that started the scene whirling. Only Rae's beautiful smile kept me from losing the hold of gravity, anchoring my mind and my sanity to solid ground. I looked towards the beach and that's when the water roared in such a formidable wave as to scatter the flamingos and pelicans as hundreds of stingrays leapt ashore. The stingrays flapped their wing-like fins resembling living pancakes with sharp pointed tails, hopping across the sand towards Rae's hammock. Wave after wave brought more stingrays from the ocean up onto the sand. I tried to back away from their sharp dangerous tails but Rae's glance at me held me in place. The brown and gray stingrays swung their poisonous stingers on the end of their long tails like coach whips. The stingrays hopped like grounded bats with scorpion tails curling, surrounding Rae and I. Suddenly the stingrays charged in a massive smothering pack into us and I was knocked backwards on the sand. I watched in horror as Rae held out her arms and let the hopping stingrays sting her skin with their poison tails. Stingrays hopped over others to get their chance to sting her, to inject their poison barbed tails into her smooth defenseless skin. Rae stood there, letting each stingray inject her and then hop back towards the water. She endured each sting with only a slight grimace as finally the last stingray popped his stinger into her shoulder and dashed into the surf. I stared, disbelieving at what I had just witnessed. Rae stood motionless with a strange far away look on her face. Her dress was ripped into shreds of material. I could see hundreds of red welts all over her skin. Her arms, legs, neck and belly were swelling and turning scarlet. The stingrays had spared her face but seemed to have left nowhere else untouched. Rae looked at me and started to smile, and then she fell over on her side in the sand.

I reached down for her and held her head up. The flocks of birds began to sing and chatter and squawk. The noise from the birds drowned out the sound of the crashing surf and Rae opened her sparkling eyes and spoke to me, "I love you."

Her eyes closed and her head fell back. I could feel her soft hair blowing in the wind around my fingers and I tried to shake her head gently to wake her. I looked around and all the birds were gone. I was alone on the beach with Rae. The sky had turned a deep mysterious gray and I could see one bright point of light, a far away star twinkling in the vastness. I stood up and stared at the star. I remember waking up then and it was only about three a.m. I got up and put on my shorts, quietly going outside through the front door. I thought about Rae leaving and about the dream. I looked up into the blue-purple sky stretched out over Santa Fe, Texas. I realized that there were too many stars and I could never find the one star that was shining in my dream. I sat in our chair swing in the front yard and thought about Rae. I looked up at the stars but my mind could only see her face. I thought about this place, this neighborhood on this dead end street in this small cow pasture town and I thought about Rae out there in the world someday seeking a new life. I never even thought of myself anywhere but here.

"...HEY WHAT IF THERE IS A HERD OF LOST WHITE-TAILED DEER..."

I didn't see Rae very much in the next few weeks because I was busy playing sports and she was back to her usual reclusive status. Finally on a crisp Saturday morning I saw her walking out into the cow pastures behind her house. I was on the barn roof with my bird book spotting red-tailed hawks and turkey vultures soaring on the air currents in a cloudless sky. I remember that day being the most solid blue sky I had ever seen. If it weren't for the hawks and vultures soaring like distant black silhouettes, the sky would have been sheer and spotless blue. Rae walked delicately through the tall brown grass, making her way around the bull nettles and sticker brush. I heard someone shout behind me, "Hey! Come here!"

It was Kenny Bulbear and Terry from across the street. Terry said, "C'mon down and lets go hiking. I heard from Mikey Mack that a herd of white-tailed deer is moving over near Cemetery Road."

I rolled my eyes as I began to climb down. I jumped off the tin of the barn roof and tumbled on the ground scattering about a dozen of my dad's chickens. I hated that these guys were interrupting my visions of Rae. When I stood up I said, "Mikey Mack? You believe anything Mikey Mack says? C'mon Terry, remember last time Mikey Mack told you about that guy who had an African Cape buffalo in a pen at his house over on the other side of the rice canal. We rode our bikes forever and it took us all day to get there just to see this huge buffalo. Just 'cuz you believed Mikey Mack. We got to the place and it was a dump. It was a rusty old broken down trailer house with a muddy corral out back. Remember that big African Cape buffalo standing there in mud up to his knees. Yeah buffalo! Hah! Mikey Mack lied again! We spent our whole day journeying to see a buffalo and we end up looking at a mistreated black Mexican steer."

Terry laughed but he agreed, saying, "Yeah, you're right, Mikey Mack tells stories but hey what if there is a lost herd of white-tailed deer back up in those pastures? I think we could go catch us one and raise it with the cows. Catching a deer would be cool. We could do it too. I got a plan."

Kenny Bulbear asked, "Plan? What kind of plan? Heck, I bet your plan is stupid like you. You probably think we can get a big shrimp net and hold it out while you chase the deer right into it."

I laughed and said, "Okay, Terry, what kind of plan?"

He gave Kenny a mean look but got excited as he started his explanation, "The plan is this, we get some ropes and surround the deer. Then we throw the ropes on a buck with antlers. If we get three ropes on a big buck we can pull in different directions and control it. We then tire it out and drag it back to the barn and tie it up in a stall."

I didn't have a better plan and I was sure Mikey Mack was lying anyway so I just shrugged my shoulders and said, "I'm in."

In a short time, equipped with three ropes and Terry had insisted on bringing his twenty-two rifle, we headed out north towards the pastures near Cemetery Road. I glanced out towards where Rae had been walking but she was gone.

An hour later we were in the Jannik's vast pasture only

about a few miles from Cemetery Road. The abandoned old cemetery, overgrown with weeds and brush, was still two miles north of here near the Dickinson Bayou. We sat down under a stand of tallow trees in a pasture dotted with huge ten-foot tall clumps of thorn bushes. We had seen a few cattle but didn't get any trouble from range bulls. We hadn't seen any deer yet. I had been searching the ground for their tracks but there was no sign to be found. While we were resting and thinking about a herd of white-tailed deer I heard something moving towards us. Looking up, we were surprised as Kenny's dog, Grizzly, came running towards us. That dog must have been following our trail all day. We all stood up as the German Shepherd ran to us but he didn't stop. He started barking. He ran past us and our eyes followed him.

Our eyes opened wide as we saw the dog barking at a herd of deer. The deer immediately turned and leapt, running off in all directions. One big buck with huge wicked antlers turned and faced Grizzly. The buck deer lowered its head and thrashed its antlers at the growling, barking dog. Terry got up and said, "C'mon, now's our chance. Circle the deer and get your ropes ready!"

Everything was happening fast. We all ran and got positions around the deer, closing in from all sides while Grizzly cut off the buck each time it tried to run. We looped our ropes and got ready to lasso the buck's antlers. Terry counted out loud, "One, two three..."

Terry and Kenny tossed their ropes towards the deer's antler but both ropes fell short. I didn't throw mine yet but I crept closer to the deer as it lowered its head and charged the barking dog. Suddenly the buck changed its mind and wheeled in a circle away from Grizzly and charged directly at me. I raised my rope preparing to loop it over the antlers. Grizzly dashed in and bit the deer in the rear leg. The buck stopped in front of me, afraid of the rope and kicking the dog off of its leg. That is when I did a stupid thing.

I heard Kenny yell, "Grab him!"

Instead of roping the buck, I dropped the rope and grabbed the deer with both hands on both antlers. I think the deer was so surprised that at first it just stood there. It seemed like everything stopped, like time was frozen. I could hear my heart pounding and the buck's wild eyes rolled as it looked at me. I felt the strength in the buck's neck as it started to resist my pull on its antlers. I yelled at Terry and Kenny, "Help me!"

They charged in from both sides but that's what startled the deer even more. Instead of resisting my pull on its antlers the buck lowered its head and charged into me. If I would have held onto the deer another split second the buck would had transfixed my chest with a pare of sharp pointed antlers. The deer could easily have killed me. Remembering back, I had wondered if they would have put a rack of deer antlers on my tombstone. My gravestone would have read: "R.I.P. This boy was stupidly killed by a deer."

When the buck charged me I let go and fell. The angered buck leapt over my falling body and I felt his rear hoof clip me on the side of the head, knocking my cap off. Grizzly barked ferociously and took off running after the fleeing buck. That's when Terry aimed his rifle and tried to shoot the escaping deer. I hollered, "Don't!"

He fired anyway and knocked a brown sparrow off a tree branch, snapping the branch into two pieces. The sparrow got up and flew away. I guess the bird got away lucky. Terry and Kenny ran up to me asking if I was okay. I turned to look and watched the jumping, running deer disappearing into the thick brush. I continued to hear Grizzly barking for several minutes after that. I stood up and felt my head where the deer's hoof had hit me. I wasn't bleeding but I had a small knot pop up and I rubbed the spot. Kenny said, "Hey, why didn't you just get the rope on him? You must be crazy trying to wrestle a deer like a steer."

Terry wiped some dead leaves from my back and chimed in, "Yeah, what the heck were you thinking? You wanted to become the famous deer wrangler of Santa Fe? Thanks to your dumb deer wrestling we didn't catch any at all. If you would have used the rope like the plan, we might have caught the buck."

I yelled back, "Yeah! Plan? The plan! I guess I forgot about the plan! Hey let's go chase down a herd of deer and rope a buck. Next time why don't we go rope a cougar or maybe a wolf? Oh, wait they don't have antlers, how about a big longhorn bull? Tomorrow let's get your plan and go rope one of Mr. Fiddion's longhorn bulls out in his pasture. Talk about dumb, trying to shoot the deer? Even if you hit it, what then? Were we going to drag the buck back to the house and make deer sausage? Oh, I get it, maybe you just wanted the antler rack? At least you missed, heck, you even missed the sparrow but at least you hit the tree branch. Look, I can't help what happened. I thought I could hold the deer by the antlers until you two roped it. I didn't count on it being that strong or dangerous. Who ever thought of deer as dangerous?"

They both shrugged their shoulders like Larry and Curly of the Three Stooges and Terry said, "Okay so the plan didn't work. But C'mon, tell me it wasn't fun."

I said, "Okay it wasn't fun."

But I laughed and thought to myself that it had been fun now that I didn't get stabbed with a deer antler. We all three walked back towards the pastures close to home. We always had great conversations on those walks in the pastures. Kenny asked, "Were you scared when the buck tried to stab you?"

Of course I wouldn't admit fear to my buddies or anyone else, except maybe my mom, so I said, "Are you crazy? Scared? Of what? A deer? C'mon, I grab cottonmouth snakes with my bare-hands and you think I might have been scared of a deer? Wake up boy!"

I said, "Is Tarzan scared of fighting a lion with just a knife? Is Superman scared of anything? Well, maybe Superman is a little worried about green Kryptonite but is Spiderman scared of the Green Goblin? Heck no! So I can tell you I ain't scared of a buck deer or a cottonmouth water moccasin!"

Kenny replied, "Well, I ain't scared of a deer either but I ain't gonna' catch a cotton-mouth or a rattlesnake with my bare hands!"

Terry chimed in, "Yeah, maybe you catch water moccasins and maybe you ain't scared of a deer but I saw Tarzan once get captured by the Leopard People and I think I could tell he was scared for a minute. Tarzan was tied up in a hut with some other safari people and outside the hut the evil native Leopard People were tying captured people up to two poles. Did ya'll see that one where they would cut a rope and the two poles would spring apart ripping the tied up people in half! That was gross! Tarzan was worried but he sent the chimp, Cheetah, to go and get Simba, the elephant. The elephants came charging through and saved everybody, or something like that. Maybe I'm getting two Tarzan movies mixed up but you know what I mean."

I laughed and said, "Yep, you are getting the Tarzan episodes mixed up but the Leopard People were probably the most dangerous to Tarzan except maybe the people from the city of gold, Opar, where the Amazon women lived. But like I said, Tarzan wasn't afraid. Once I saw him attack a wild rampaging rhinoceros. Tarzan was dodging the charging rhinoceros and then he jumped on it's back and stabbed it with his knife. Now, that was real too, they didn't use a stunt man or a fake rhino either."

Terry frowned and thought for a moment before saying, "Well, maybe you ain't afraid of a buck deer but you are afraid of Rae Kimmings."

Everything got quiet. We walked in silence and the only sound was the slight wind in the trees and the swishing of our legs in the tall brown grass of the pastures. I couldn't reply. They both knew it was true. Finally I said, "Yeah, it was fun trying to catch that deer, you guys, but maybe we should stick to catching snakes."

We got back to our barn and I searched the fields for Rae as we walked, but she was gone. Terry and Kenny went home and I walked slowly back out to the barn to feed the chickens and watch them peck at the chicken scratch. I climbed up into the big tallow tree overlooking the chicken yard out by the barn and sat in the big crotch. It was always so comfortable up there and you could see almost as far as on top of the barn. I sat there watching the sun slowly get lower in the west Texas sky. The chickens pecked noisily and every once in while a big yellow-necked black rooster would crow sporadically. I searched the fading light of the sky for the first flying nighthawk of the approaching evening. I heard a meadowlark singing a prairie opera far out in the pasture. I sat up in that tree replaying the event with the deer and how I would have rather stayed and talked to Rae than go out chasing a deer herd.

As I sat in the tree thinking, I heard something in the branches above me. I guessed the chickens must have already started flying up in the tree to get ready for their nightly roost. I searched the tops of the tree and saw that the noise wasn't a chicken. About ten feet higher than I sat was a young opossum climbing along a thin branch. My dad would shoot the opossum if he saw him. He said that opossum's ate the chicken's eggs. One time he killed one with a baseball bat. That wasn't a pretty sight, in fact I was there and got splattered with the opossum blood and when I went back to the house to wash off, my mom screamed and thought I was bleeding. I smiled as I watched this smallish opossum slowly climbing in the tree. He wasn't even paying any attention to me as if he knew I wasn't a threat. Most people think opossums are ugly and that they look like big white and gray rats but I think they are interesting and friendly looking. They are sort of like dolphins in the way it looks like they are always smiling. Dolphins and opossums are the most smiling animals on earth.

I thought about going up higher in the tree and maybe catching the opossum but it would be getting dark soon and I decided to not bother him. I climbed down from the tree and headed back to the house. I glanced in the direction of Rae's house and saw the porch light on. Rae was sitting on the porch swing reading. I missed talking to her, seeing her, but I also was afraid of seeing her because of my promise to help her leave. I guess I figured if I didn't see her I wouldn't have to help her leave and then maybe she would have to stay. A nighthawk buzzed my head and I instinctively ducked. Rae sensed my approach and looked up from her book. I asked, as I got closer, "What are you reading this time?"

Rae looked up and her smile seemed to shine like that distant star from my dream. Seeing her smile that way at me I almost just stopped walking towards her and stood still. Rae's smile was like a warming heat covering my skin and rippling inside my heart. At that moment I almost cried thinking of her leaving. I didn't think I could bear never seeing her again. Terry was right, I was afraid of her but I was more afraid of never seeing her again. I had never been in love and I didn't even know what love was but Rae was mysteriously pulling my heart and I had never felt anything this powerful before. When Rae smiled at me that night I knew something inside of me had changed forever. I was in love with Rae Kimmings. I was in love with her and she didn't even know. She was leaving and I had to help her go. Maybe I should just go and cut my own heart out and mail it to Alaska. That is what this was starting to feel like. Love was not a good thing to me. This wasn't love like in the movies. This wasn't Tarzan and Jane or Superman and Lois or Peter Parker and Mary Jane or even Romeo and Juliet. This was more like Cinderella and the Prince that takes the glass slipper and moves away never to see Cinderella again.

Rae had a radio playing beside her and I could hear John Denver singing Annie's Song. I still remember those lyrics, "*You fill up my senses like a night in the forest, like the mountains in springtime, like a walk in the rain...Come let me love you, let me give my life to you, let me drown in your laughter, let me die in your arms...*"

That song at that time filled me up and it was how I felt standing there in Rae's yard, ten feet away from her reading on the porch swing. I let the music from the radio seep into my heart and I felt more emotion in that instant than I probably had ever in my young life. Rae looked so beautiful sitting in the swing with her blonde soft hair strewn about her shoulders. In my mind, twenty-five years later, I can still recall exactly how she looked sitting in that swing on the night that I decided not to catch an opossum in the tree.

After I asked what she was reading she smiled at me and then closed her book holding it up so that I could see the cover, replying, "You might think this is silly but I am reading "The Animal Story Book." This book was published in 1953. I found it stuck way back in the shelves of my dad's library. It is very good. It has many stories by good writers like: Rudyard Kipling, Robert Cochrane, Robert Browning, William Blake, and even Aesop's fables. My favorite piece in the book is the one by William Blake, "The Tiger." He wrote it somewhere in the early 1800's I think. Have you ever read it? You know the one that reads, "Tiger! Tiger! Burning bright, in the forest of the night?"

I just stuttered a bit and said, "I think I read it before. I have heard of it, yeah about a tiger."

I said this even though I had no idea what she was talking about. I didn't want to always seem so clueless when it came to the books she read. Rae smiled and continued on about the book, "I just love reading Aesop's fables about animals. They teach such cool things. I really like the one called, "The Fox and the Crow. There is this crow sitting on a low branch with a big piece of cheese in her beak. A fox comes along and spies the cheese and the crow and says, "Mistress Crow, you are beautiful. You have pretty glossy feathers and pretty eyes and I know that indeed your voice must be beautiful too. Could you please sing me a pretty song?" Well, the crow opens her beak to sing and the cheese falls into the waiting mouth of the fox. The fox said, "That will do, that was all I wanted."

In exchange for the cheese, the fox gave her a piece of advice, "Do not trust flatterers." I love that! At the end, it has like this ancient proverb or something that says, "The flatterer doth rob by stealth, His victim, both of wit and wealth." Don't you think that is so cool?"

She moved over on the swing and patted a spot besides her, saying, "Come over here and sit down."

I was thinking about that proverb Rae just told me and as I sat down I said, "Rae, does that mean if someone tells you that you are beautiful that you don't believe it and then you don't trust that person?"

She laughed a bit, and chuckling still said, "You are a silly fox, I guess but remember I am not a vain miss crow."

After she said that Mr. Kimmings came out of the garage and waved "hello" to me. "Hi, how are you, Mr. Kimmings? When are you going after snapping turtles again?"

He took his cap off and scratched his head, replying, "Well, I've been thinking probably in another couple of weeks. I would love to have your help again."

I nodded, and said, "Just let me know, I'll be glad to go again."

Mr. Kimmings nodded back and said, "Rae, you don't stay out here too long you've got things to catch up on in the house. Goodnight, you two, I've got to get to sleep. I have an early start at work tomorrow."

Mr. Kimmings went inside and Rae turned off the radio. We sat on the swing in silence for a few minutes. I remember how loud the crickets sounded out there in the darkness. That was the only sound I could hear, besides my heartbeat, which seemed louder than the army of over a million cricket singers. Rae was looking south in the darkness and I was looking at her beautiful blue-green eyes. The flecks in her eyes seemed like someone broke a green and blue stained glass window in a cathedral and scattered the scintillating shards there. I was mesmerized and emotions poured inside of me along every artery and vein. Instead of blood, my heart pumped pure emotion. I wanted to kiss Rae at that moment.

She turned to look at me and saw me staring. She didn't say anything but looked deeply into my eyes as if searching for the truth of what lies at my core. I saw her lips slowly open and I knew I had to kiss her. I leaned forward and she leaned towards me. Our lips met slowly like the breeze pushing two grapes together, growing on the same vine. We kissed without breathing and my hand found the soft skin of her face and my fingers crept up into her cascading hair. We pulled each other closer as we kissed intensely. My body underwent electrical shocks and synaptic responses firing like a showering of sparks from a thousand transformers exploding. I didn't want the kiss to end. I didn't dare to breathe for fear of never breathing again. I let everything inside of me go into another realm. I gave myself over to the emotions that pulled me to Rae.

We ended our kiss and stared at each other, sitting on that squeaky swing on her front porch. I didn't want to speak and ruin the moment but Rae finally sighed and touched my face with her soft hand. I will never forget the tender touch of her hand to my face. She blinked her eyes rapidly, and I saw a tear form as she said, "That was so wonderful. You have been such a beautiful person to me, always. I know I haven't always responded to you but I have had my reasons. I wanted to kiss you more than anything many times. You know I am leaving and you have promised to help me, but I can't make you. You don't have to help me leave. Thank you for your unwavering friendship. Kissing you was the best kiss I have ever felt, and I truly mean that. I will never forget you and maybe life will choose us to cross paths again someday."

I continued to look deep into her eyes as she spoke. My mind reeled as the truth of what she was telling me began to sink in like concrete setting up in the hot sun. The intense feeling of love and passion from our kiss shattered into a panic of reality when I heard and assimilated what Rae was explaining to me. I couldn't believe she still wanted to leave. I loved her and she had to feel something for me. How could she still want to leave? I was panicking on the inside and I could feel tears starting to flow. I was so choked up I couldn't speak. I stood up and stared at her in disbelief. I pleaded, "But, Rae...why now? You can leave later, months, years from now, the Florida Keys will still be there."

I heard the front door open and Mr. Kimmings said, "Rae, it's time to come in."

She stood up and hugged me tightly and then stepped back holding both my hands in hers, saying, "It will be okay...we are both just starting our lives. Remember we will both have to find our true path when the roads fork in many directions. I'm sure life has many gifts for you and we will both find our destiny entwined down the road. Always I will keep you in my heart."

She kissed me on my lips again and that quick kiss burned like scalding fire. I wanted to tell her I loved her but the kiss burned and my mind was numb. Rae was gone inside her house before I realized and I was still standing there by the swing when the porch light was turned off.

I couldn't get to sleep that night. I could still feel her kisses and the memory flamed my heart. I had never before felt anything as powerful or as painful. Love was the sweetest, most obsessive, emotion and I was finding out that it could be the most blissful event or the most excruciating torture. No wonder the Eskimos have about twenty something different words for love. I kept thinking that if I told Rae I loved her she wouldn't leave. I would have to stop her. Then I would think, what if I told her I loved her and she still left? I was consumed with worry and doubt. I don't know what time I fell asleep but I know it was probably almost morning by the time I finally found deep slumber.

"A SMALL PHOTO FELL ONTO MY LAP."

Rae was gone. She left a long letter on her dad's desk to explain her disappearance. My mom told me he wasn't taking her leaving very well. I know he tried to find her and she did call quite often to let them know she was doing well. He finally found out she was with her great aunt and relaxed more. She tried to make him understand it wasn't his fault. She told him it was something she had to do. He worried about her but over time he knew that his daughter was a different sort of independent and atypical young woman. She wrote me a long letter about a month later. I remember coming home from school and my mom handing me the letter. I went outside to sit on top of the barn to read it. I wanted to imagine that she was out there in the pasture sitting in the tall brown grass while I read her words to me. In my memory I could still see her sitting Indian style on the ground with honeybees buzzing nearby and white cattle egrets striding around her in the pasture. I opened her letter with nervous fingers and unfolded the paper. A small photo fell onto my lap. I looked at the picture of Rae on a clean sandy beach with a wide expansive ocean of blue-green water behind her. The water was like the color of the depths of her eyes. Rae was sitting on a huge piece of driftwood wearing a yellow summer dress and holding a book. She looked happy and complete. Her smile was like a special phenomenon. I had never seen Rae smile with such truth revealed in her face. As much as I missed her and still loved her I knew this is where she was meant to be.

Her letter was written in blue ink with her large circular style of up and down writing. Rae always wrote her letters with an artsy flowing style. She usually only put about four words to a line because each word was written so large and round. She had beautiful penmanship. She started the letter off with my nickname, which I thought was unusual, but endearing to me.

My sweet Cottontop,
I miss you. I am happy down here in the Florida Keys. I wanted to write this letter to you to tell you that I am sorry if I ever caused you any pain. I never meant to but that night we kissed I knew I had hurt you. I wanted to kiss you so much for my own selfish reasons but I wouldn't give that moment back for anything. I know my leaving hurt other people too but I had a choice to make for my life and it was hard and painful. I know it was tough on my parents, especially dad. Please keep him company and go snapping turtle fishing with him. I miss the tall brown grass of the cow pastures to read in but the beach and the ocean is more home to me. I have always felt like I belonged here and now I have found out how true that was. I came here because my great aunt lives here and I live in a trailer, that she owns, behind her house for now. I go to school and work a couple of nights a week at the library. I have made a new friend named, Marci Jhillian. She is in the botanist club and we go out and look up plants we find in the books at the library. Aren't we so very boring? Ha, ha! I was reminded of you and my dad the other day when I was out walking near the marshes and saw a huge snapping turtle, with his neck stretched out long, walking slowly between ponds of water. I knew you would have tried to catch him

and I could just imagine you here chasing a snapping turtle through the swamp. I know it's a good thing you aren't down here because you would be trying to catch alligators and there are hundreds of them everywhere. I swim in the ocean at least twice a week and the water is warm and pleasant. Time truly does seem slower here. The days last longer and the nights are shorter. I love just being out near the ocean, listening to the waves rolling in and watching the hundreds of different kinds of birds. This place is like bird heaven! You would just die to see so many birds. The air here is better to breathe too. The sky at night is black and purple, filled with more stars than in Santa Fe. You would love it here. Someday you must come to the Florida Keys and visit. You could go all the way down to Key West and then up to Bahia Honda and Marathon. Maybe someday I will come back to old Santa Fe to visit for a holiday. You will always be my best friend! I miss you and stay true to your destiny!

Hugs and Kisses XXXOOOXXX
Rae Kimmings

The letter was shaking in my hands as I looked at the photo of Rae. Tears rolled down my cheeks. I still loved her. I vowed to someday go to the Florida Keys to see what the great attraction was. Could there be other places in the world better than Santa Fe, Texas? This place was all I had ever known. I loved the endless pastures, the huge sticker bushes, the flat white sand where giant red ants made their homes, the rice canals of the nutria, alligator gar, and the common snapping turtle, the bayou that ran like a sluggish snake through thickets where raccoons, armadillos, and opossums lived. I sat there on the tin roof of the barn that my dad had built for cows and chickens and reread Rae's letter over and over again. Tears fell from my eyes blurring some of the ink of her words on the letter. I missed her and I couldn't imagine how I would ever stop missing her. It was like I could still see her blue-green eyes in the sky before me. I will always be able to envision her sitting out there, reading in the cow pasture with her long blonde hair blowing like a flame in the wind, like it was just yesterday. I still see Rae in my mind and in my heart, even though it was over thirty years ago. I can still see Rae Kimmings.

EPILOGUE

I still live in Galveston County in Texas and have never lived anywhere else in my entire life. Santa Fe is the farthest city on the west side of Galveston County. The next city is Alvin but that crosses the county line into Brazoria County. I have lived here my entire life and it is doubtful I will ever live anywhere else. Rae experienced other worlds, other places, and I guess she always had a gypsy's heart. I realized many years later that destiny would not reunite us. Rae had that figured out long ago. I still loved her like the way you look back and yearn for your lost youth. You can never get it back but you can never forget it either. Life took us in two different directions and we each found our own way. She was always a reader and I somehow became a writer. I never really saw her again. A couple of times during the Christmas holidays when I went home to my parent's house I heard she was visiting her parent's house but for some strange reason I never went down the street to visit. I intended to go see her but I also was afraid, as if seeing her would cause me pain or maybe seeing her would ruin my memory of her. I missed my opportunities because life has a way of sweeping you along like a rapid river. If you stay in the current you miss many things along the side of the river. I have since learned to grab at rocks and slow the current of the river so that I may get out and walk around on the shore.

A few years ago I decided to write this book to her. I was going to see her and give her the completed manuscript as a kind of gift to our youth and the memory of what we shared as teens. I finished the first few chapters and set it aside to begin writing other books. The Honey Bee Girl was kept hidden away in a folder as I wrote many other books. I had meant to go back and finish it but I never did, consumed with spewing out words of fiction and poetry.

I heard from my mom that she had finally gotten married. I heard that maybe she had moved back to Galveston but I wasn't sure. I was glad that she had found a happy life. There was that day in 1999 when I got a telephone call from my mom. She told me the news. Rae was gone. She had died from Hepatitis in a Galveston hospital. She was only forty-one years old.

Following her last wishes her ashes were scattered in the Gulf of Mexico over the waves. When I go to the beach in Galveston and I stare out across the water I think about Rae. I put my hands in my pockets and the wind brushes gently at my neck like the way her fingers felt against my cheek. I sometimes take out that last photo of Rae in the Florida Keys and wonder what would have happened, if I had told her, that I loved her.

Santa Fe isn't the same as it was back in 1973. It will never be like that again. Rae and I were drawn together in 1973 and she left and you can never get that same feeling back again. I remember how Santa Fe was then and I remember Rae back then. I can only go back with the fading images in my mind to a place when life was easy and the sky held the mysteries of our future. I remember the lesson of the marsh hawk with the broken wing and how some things never heal. We each followed our dreams to different places. My dreams take me on trips into my imagination to places never before seen and her dreams led her away from me. Rae is gone and I never told her what was in my heart. I wonder if she knows it now.

Doug Hiser is an author of several books and a professional artist. He is from southern Texas and was born to catch cottonmouth water moccasin snakes and grab armadillos by the tail. His life involves nature, sports, and traveling to wilderness places that are still left on the globe.